# DEDICATION

For my mother, Ruby,
who sailed the Pacific Ocean
in the sailboat my dad, John, built.
She passed on her Spirit of
Adventure to me and my siblings,
Rebecca, Joan and Johnny.
Ruby taught us all
how to have fun!

# MEET ME AT MIDNIGHT

Nate Robbins needs the money bequeathed to him by his eccentric uncle — but in order to get it he must remarry before his thirtieth birthday, three weeks away. Deserted by her husband, Samantha Feldon is determined not to marry again unless she's sure the love she finds is true. So when her boss — Nate Robbins — offers her the job of 'wife', she refuses, but agrees to help him find someone suitable. Accompanying him on a Caribbean cruise, Sam finds him the perfect woman — realizing too late she loves Nate herself . . .

GAEL MORRISON

# MEET ME AT MIDNIGHT

**LINFORD**
*Leicester*

First published in Great Britain in 2012

First Linford Edition
published 2015

*A catalogue record for this book is available
from the British Library.*

ISBN 978–1–4448–2660–9

Published by
F. A. Thorpe (Publishing)
Anstey, Leicestershire

Set by Words & Graphics Ltd.
Anstey, Leicestershire
Printed and bound in Great Britain by
T. J. International Ltd., Padstow, Cornwall

This book is printed on acid-free paper

# 1

'You want me to do what?' Samantha Feldon demanded, incredulity battling outrage in her wide blue eyes. A strand of blonde hair escaped its hairslide and fluttered across her suddenly pink cheek.

'Marry me,' Nate Robbins repeated. He firmly squashed the memories of the woman to whom he had last uttered those words. To Jenny, his wife.

'Marry you!'

Nate nodded. Uncle Edward may have forced the issue, but he had in the end agreed. All he needed now was for his assistant to do the same.

'Have you lost your mind?' Sam gazed at him pityingly.

Nate shifted from his usual comfortable sprawl and leaned forward so his elbows rested on his desk. He frowned as Sam raked her hair back from her face and her eyes deepened to the colour of sea in a storm.

She didn't look as though she were about to say yes, but he hadn't built a successful business by faltering in the face of opposition. Sam would come around. As soon as he made it clear how it would be a good thing.

'I need a wife,' he said. 'You will do nicely.'

'Do?' she repeated. The pink on her cheeks deepened to red.

'You're not married,' he went on.

'No,' she said slowly, but her eyes lost their wide look, narrowing in an instant to a laser pinpoint of light.

'You're unattached.' He had noted no young man collecting his assistant after work, or interrupting her during dictation with lovesick phone calls. She must care no more than he for love or passion and the pain that came when love and passion ended.

Sam didn't reply. She simply stared at him steadily with a disconcerting gaze.

'That's all right then,' he said, frowning.

'It's not all right.'

He shifted his gaze to his desk diary, pretending not to hear what she had said. 'How about the twenty-eighth of December?'

'No,' Sam said firmly.

He cast her a swift glance and cursed himself for being a fool. He had hurried her, that was all. Despite the fact that this marriage wouldn't be usual, women still needed time to prepare. Jenny had taken months.

His shoulders tensed. Sam was nothing like Jenny, a fact for which he'd been grateful when Sam began working for him. He needed no reminders to conjure up images of his wife. They were there in his head and in his heart.

'The twenty-eighth is a good day,' he went on, knowing that if he didn't he might stop altogether. 'Christmas will be over and it's not too close to New Year's Eve.'

'No.' Sam stood.

Nate got to his feet also. 'What's wrong?' he asked.

She remained standing opposite as though frozen into position, and for a long moment he studied her eyes. Saw the light there, the softness, and behind the softness, the strength.

'I don't know how you can expect — ' Her words suddenly snagged as though blocked by a tight throat.

Why couldn't she react as she usually did, doing what he asked with a minimum of fuss? He'd thought this plan through. Why couldn't she simply trust him?

'It's business,' he said, not wanting to explain that there was more to it than that. 'We'll both benefit by marrying.'

She didn't sink into her chair as he'd hoped she would, but continued to gaze at him as though he'd gone insane.

Nate pressed his lips together. It wasn't as though *he* wanted marriage either. He had fought the notion for almost a year. He didn't want another wife. Not after Jenny.

'Forget it,' he growled.

'Forget it!' she repeated, her voice high and strained. 'You ask me to be your wife then you tell me to forget it?'

He felt suddenly weary. He should have known better than to suggest any such thing. Women forgot nothing. Jenny had stored details as she would dollars in a bank, ready to bring them out when the occasion arose.

'Are you in trouble?' Sam asked, her voice suddenly gentler. Her eyes were gentler too, as though she were trying to understand.

Nate's shoulders stiffened. He was damned if he was going to admit he was in trouble, that if Sam didn't marry him, his business was finished. The business he'd built up in honor of Jenny. He'd sworn to protect it and the people who worked for him. His employees depended on him. He had to keep them safe.

'Why a wife?' Sam went on, stepping

towards him. Her scent wafted around him like a mist in tropical air. 'Why now?'

He didn't want to explain, didn't want to speak of Uncle Edward and his will.

'Well?' Sam persisted.

He didn't want Sam to know how precarious the situation was, but from the way her chin jutted stubbornly out, it was obvious he had to tell her something.

'Because of my uncle,' he replied.

'Who?' Bewilderment showed in her eyes.

'Great-uncle Edward,' Nate replied. 'He died a few months ago.'

The confusion in her eyes cleared. 'Hasn't it been almost a year?'

He could hardly believe it had been that long. The pain was still so fresh. Despite his uncle's crazy notions, he missed the old man almost as much as he missed Jenny.

The blue satin of Sam's eyes turned to velvet. 'You lived with him, didn't you, when you were little?'

'Off and on.' More on than off. He had lived with Uncle Edward longer than with his own parents.

Sam's brow puckered. 'I don't understand what your uncle has got to do with you getting married?'

Jenny had been the one who had commanded Nate's uncle to help Nate move on. 'He put it in his will,' Nate spat out through gritted teeth.

'What do you mean?' Sam asked.

Nate rolled his shoulders, tried to force away the tension. 'Other than an annuity to Mrs. Mulroy and Samson, my uncle's housekeeper and gardener, he left everything to me — his house and twenty million dollars.'

'But that's wonderful!'

'No, it's not.'

'Why not?'

'There's a condition attached.' For what seemed the millionth time Nate cursed that condition, wishing to hell his uncle hadn't listened to Jenny and instead had done something else with his money. Even if it meant leaving it to Nate's parents, who had neglected the old man when he was alive.

All his father had done when Uncle Edward died was instruct his secretary to send flowers, and his mother hadn't communicated anything at all. She had simply carried on doing what she'd been doing since his parents' divorce, flitting from one vacation spot to the next with the latest in a stream of boyfriends.

'What sort of condition?' Sam's question dragged Nate back from unwelcome memories.

'I'm to get married,' he replied, his heart rebelling at the thought, 'before I turn thirty.'

Which was why he had asked her, Sam realized with a jolt. She'd been right to squelch the joy tumbling through her soul when Nate had asked her for her hand. His proposition was about money, not about love.

She fought back the disappointment still lingering from that moment, erased, too, a sudden fantasy of Nate on his knees before her.

'Your birthday's only three weeks away,' she said, frowning.

'How do you know when my birthday is?'

Her cheeks flushed with heat. 'It's in the personnel file. Everyone's is.' But Nate's was the only birthday, with the exception of her son's and grandmother's, that she'd marked in her birthday book on the bottom shelf of her bedroom bookcase. The heat spread to her neck. 'January the first is about the easiest day in the whole year to remember.'

'It's coming up fast.'

Sam bit her lip. 'It's a strange sort of condition. Why did your uncle — '

'I don't know.'

She could tell from the guarded expression on Nate's face that he did know. He just wasn't keen to discuss it. Which was too damn bad. 'So is that why you asked me to marry you?' she demanded.

'Yes,' he replied, a muscle rippling along his jaw.

'If you accept your great-uncle's condition, you'll be marrying for money.'

'It's as good a reason as any.'

'You can't believe that!'

'Can't I?'

An ache crawled through Sam's chest. She'd been Nate's assistant for the past two years, had thought him different from other men, had believed he had principles.

She should have known better. Her marriage to Phil should have taught her never to expect anything from a man. Somehow she'd gone on hoping.

'So I take it your answer is no?' Nate demanded.

'Yes,' she whispered, pushing away the urge to touch him. 'And by yes, I mean no.'

Nate stepped from behind his desk and the moment to touch was past. Coolness misted the space between them. If only she didn't wish that she *could* marry him, but for the right reason — love.

'Then I'll have to find someone else.' Nate pursed his lips tight. 'You can help.'

Sam's pulse pounded against her temples. 'What do you mean, help?'

'Help me find a wife.' He issued the request as though it were nothing more than an instruction to place an order with their suppliers.

'People don't ask other people to find them a wife! You're perfectly capable of finding one on your own.'

'Obviously not,' he growled, 'or I wouldn't be asking you to do it.'

'What do you think I can do?' She shifted in her chair. Did he think by asking her to perform this task, she'd simply say yes to the job herself?

'You must have friends I could meet.'

'I'm not a Madam with a list of call girls on my Rolodex.'

'I don't need a list. Just one will do. You must know someone who wants to be married?'

'No, I don't.'

'There'll be a bonus in it if you come up with a good prospect.'

'A bonus would make me just like you!'

'Which is?'

'A person willing to sell her soul for money.'

His gaze shifted from hers. He seemed to weigh his next words carefully. 'People depend on me.'

'Which people?'

'Just people.' His shoulders stiffened. 'If you're willing to help, then fine. If not — '

'I'm fired?'

'I didn't say that.'

She could see fine lines newly etched around his eyes. Worry lines, she realized. She'd seen them often enough on her own face to recognize them for what they were. Concern for him welled once more in her breast.

'Why are you doing this?' she asked. 'Is it because of what Allen Peterson said?'

'What's my accountant got to do with anything?'

'He said the company needed an influx of capital to compete internationally, that unless we expand, we'll go down the tubes.' She licked her suddenly very dry lips. She, too, had been worrying since Allen had given Nate that verdict, had stared at the notes she had taken at the meeting and tried to think of some way she could help. If the company went down, she'd be going down with it. Then, how would she care for Jamie?

The thought of her eight-year-old son steadied her.

'For expansion we need money,' she continued doggedly. 'Is that why you need your uncle's inheritance? Allen said the company has borrowed all the funds it can.'

'What did you do? Memorize every word the man uttered?'

'I have it all written down.' Sam straightened her shoulders. 'If we hadn't had that fire — '

The expression in Nate's eyes forbade her to go on.

' — paid out all those salaries to people who weren't even working — '

'People have to live.'

This time she did touch him. She reached for his hand before she realized what she was doing, then, when she tried to draw away again a tingling began where his skin touched hers.

The air entering her lungs suddenly didn't seem enough.

'I know,' she whispered. 'I never told you at the time — ' She sucked in a steadying breath, and prayed that if she acknowledged what she'd felt back then, these other feelings would disappear. 'I . . . I thought you did the right thing keeping everyone on.'

'I thought you disapproved.'

'It was economic suicide. But — ' She swallowed hard. ' — in every other sense it was wonderful. Generous.'

The expression in his eyes softened.

'But something like that can kill a company,' she added.

'We're not dead yet.'

'No,' she agreed. She stared down to where her hand covered his, tried not to think about how it felt so right. 'But we will be if you don't inherit your uncle's money.' Somehow she managed to pull her fingers back, was stunned to feel the loss of his warmth.

'Which is why I need you.'

She picked up the calendar from the top of Nate's desk. 'It's already the tenth of December. There's not enough time. You'll never make it.'

'With your help, I will.'

'You've got to meet someone, fall in love and get married, all in three weeks? It's not possible!' And thank God for that, for the idea of Nate marrying turned her heart cold.

'I have no intention of falling in love,' he declared briskly.

'But — '

'That'll cut off some time.'

'You can't marry without love!'

'People do it all the time.'

'Not people like us!'

'Like us?'

'Ordinary people.' She struggled to find the right words. 'Kings and queens might marry for other considerations, but ordinary people need love if they plan to stick together for a lifetime.'

'A lifetime can be shorter than you think.' He sucked in an audible breath. 'We could make marriage work, Sam. We could — '

'I'm not marrying without love.'

'Love isn't everything.'

When she'd fallen in love with Phil she had thought that it was, but she'd discovered too late that what she felt was simply lust, and lust wasn't enough when the going got tough.

A baby hadn't been enough either. Phil had left them both without a backward glance.

'Commitment, then,' she insisted, needing him to agree. 'You have to have commitment.'

'That's what business deals are for.'

Her heart tightened in her chest. 'Marriage is more than business.'

16

'That's all it needs to be.'

'Then heaven help your wife. She's certainly not going to be me.' And heaven help her, too, for her body was trembling and she couldn't make it stop. She had to make it stop, had to cease caring for this man who felt nothing for her other than an employer's responsibility to an employee.

'Fine,' he said, 'but if you won't do it, I need you to find someone who will.'

Perhaps it would be best if she did what he asked. If he belonged to another woman, she could push him from her mind, could dispel the dreams she'd begun to dream since she'd first begun working for him. Foolish dreams, given all he'd just said.

'Fine,' she agreed slowly, putting Nate's calendar down.

*　*　*

'So,' Sam demanded, a few days later, 'how did it go?' She tried to relax, tried to stop her brow from puckering, knowing she'd be lost if she didn't maintain a proper level of aloofness. Nate might not be the man for her, but when he ran his hand distractedly through his thick black hair, something inside her melted.

'How did what go?' he asked.

'Your date.'

'Let's just say it went and leave it at that.'

'Let's not.' She didn't want to hear details of his evening with the fabulous Chrissy St. Clare, of how wonderful it had been or how beautiful Chrissy was, but if she was to help him find a wife, details were what she needed.

'Don't you have a letter to type?' Nate's fingers closed around a pen as he reached for the top paper on his desk.

'No,' Sam said, folding her arms across her chest.

'I won't have you quizzing me after every date!'

'You put me in charge, Nate.'

'My mistake!' He scowled at her from

beneath lowered brows.

She dropped into the chair opposite, his nearness as usual resulting in a familiar breathlessness. 'So,' she continued, struggling to ignore the way her heart suddenly beat faster, 'did you pick up Miss St. Clare at her house, or did you meet her at the restaurant?'

'I picked her up.'

'And then?'

'I took her to Emilio's. We had a cocktail, some dinner — crab for her, steak for me.'

'And then?'

'I took her home.'

'And then?' she whispered, ignoring the warning in his eyes.

'I said good night.'

'Did you kiss her?' Sam swallowed hard, not wanting to imagine another woman's lips on Nate's.

'That's none of your business.'

'You've made it my business.'

'Not that, I didn't.'

'Didn't you like her?'

'She's all right.'

'She's gorgeous.' Sam's words swept out unbidden, followed by a stab of jealousy that left her weak. Chrissy St. Clare was a sales representative of one of their clients and Sam had arranged the date. She had seemed the perfect answer to what Nate wanted; beautiful, soft spoken . . . available.

'Everything a man could want,' Sam added out loud.

'Then *you* marry her!' Nate growled.

'It's not me who has to.' If she ever married again, it would be for love, not money. With someone who loved her in return, someone who would stick with her through good times and bad. 'Time's running out for you. How many dates did you go on before you asked me to help?'

'How many have *you* been on in the last year?'

'This isn't about me!'

'I've been busy.'

'Everyone's busy. If you really intend to succeed in finding a wife, you have to make the time.'

Nate's eyes narrowed.

Sam hastily changed the subject. 'Your uncle's housekeeper, Mrs. Mulroy, phoned today.'

'What did she want? Is she all right?'

'She wanted to know whether you'll be coming as usual for the holidays. She said Samson picked out a terrible Christmas tree and she wants you to tell him so.'

Nate grimaced. 'Mrs. Mulroy always thinks it's wrong. Samson's trees are either too tall or too wide or don't have enough branches.'

Sam smiled.

'Mrs. Mulroy would prefer that Samson buy a cultured tree rather than go out into our back woods and chop down his own.' Nate leaned back in his chair. 'What did you tell her?'

'That you'd ring her back.'

'I'll do it later. Now let's get to work.'

'We haven't finished discussing this marriage thing yet. One week's already gone by and you've only dated one person.' She pressed her lips together.

'We have to settle on a game plan.'

'You're in charge.' He shrugged. 'Do your worst.'

'I've done my best with no results. I don't know what else to do.'

'You could marry me yourself.'

She turned away, was afraid the intensity of his gaze would force her to do what he wanted. 'I can't,' she said firmly, then looked up once more. 'And I don't understand why you haven't dealt with this earlier.'

'Are you saying it's impossible?'

'Nothing's impossible. Not if it's something you want badly enough.'

'It's not a question of wanting.'

'Well you had better start wanting. Think about why you're doing this. People depend on you. I ... '

Somehow Sam managed to stop before she said anything more. She didn't want anyone, especially her boss, to know how much she feared losing her job. For if she lost it, everything she had worked so hard to achieve in the past eight years would come crashing down around her. Then where would her son be?

'What happens, Nate, if you don't marry on time?'

'My uncle's estate goes elsewhere.'

'Where?'

'To a local historical society he's been supporting.'

Sam caught her breath, unable to believe she had heard correctly. Would the business Nate had worked so hard to establish slide into bankruptcy because his inheritance had gone to a society that cared more for the past than the future?

She couldn't allow that to happen. Somehow she'd have to ensure Nate succeeded in his quest, yet at the same time manage to keep him at arm's length. It wouldn't be easy. The last time she had allowed herself to feel this strongly about a man, she had wound up pregnant.

She gritted her jaw. 'You have to put yourself out there.'

'Out where?' he asked.

'Wherever women are looking for men.'

'I'm not looking. As far as I'm concerned, you're my ideal choice.'

'I'm not available.'

'Well, I'm not cruising bars.' With that pronouncement Nate jabbed the end of his pencil into the electric sharpener.

'That's it!' Sam exclaimed.

'What's it?'

'Cruising — a cruise.' She raised her voice to be heard over the whir of the sharpener. 'Tropical nights, warm seas, single women looking for romance.'

The whirring stopped. Nate looked at her thoughtfully. 'Could work,' he finally said. 'When do we leave?'

'We?' she demanded.

'I'm not going alone.'

'Well, *I'm* not going.'

'A Caribbean cruise could be just the thing.'

'For you, not for me.'

'Eastern or western Caribbean? Or maybe Hawaii?'

'Nate!'

'What?' His eyes appeared innocent as he trained his gaze on her.

'You have to go alone.'

'No, I don't. You promised to help.'

'I never promised to go on a cruise.'

'You could use a holiday.' He stood and stepped around his desk, offering her his hand and pulling her to her feet. 'You look tired,' he said.

'I have responsibilities.' If only he would step away . . . if only she could think. 'Family,' she continued desperately, 'my son, my — '

'Your son.' Her boss frowned. 'You can't leave your son at Christmas.'

He understood, Sam thought dazedly, gazing into Nate's eyes. The thought warmed her, relieved her.

'He'll have to come with us.'

'With us?' Sam cried. Her relief died as swiftly as it had been born.

'Your son will love it,' Nate said positively.

'My grandmother lives with us also.'

'You want her to come too?'

'I don't want any of them coming, because I'm not coming.' She stabbed her finger into his chest, and in that instant regretted her forward motion. She was even closer to him now, could feel his warmth, breathe his air.

Hastily, she stepped away.

'My family loves Christmas,' she went on raggedly. 'I love Christmas. We stay home, trim the tree, drink eggnog, make sugar cookies . . . That's the way we like it, the way we've always liked it. If you're going to get a bride — ' She stared at Nate sternly. ' — you're going to have to do it on your own.'

# 2

He should have guessed that Sam's home would be just like her; all warmth and light, with surprises in unexpected places. Like that turret built on the corner of the roof with no regard for symmetry or style. Just plunked there for no reason other than someone fancied it.

He should have realized Sam had this serendipitous quality to her character. All the signs were there; the photo she kept on her desk of her son aged little more than two, sprawled like a tiger the full length of a tree branch. The boy was laughing, as though daring his mother to get him down, but instead what she had done was take his picture.

Then there was her penchant for arranging wildflowers in jam jars, even though he'd gone to the trouble after the first time she'd done it, of ordering bouquets from the florist instead, complete with cut glass vases. When he had told her their clients would find her arrangements unprofessional, she had simply laughed and replied that their clients would appreciate her attempt to bring a little life into the office setting.

And she had been right. People from all over the country had commented on the flowers, and that buyer from Detroit had actually asked to take some home.

The flowers had succeeded in warming even him. Which worried him. Warmth was dangerous. Especially the warmth of a woman like Sam. A man might fall in love, might lose everything that kept him safe.

If he was wise, he would make efforts to stay away from her. Trouble was he needed Sam. And not to find some stranger who would demand more than he wanted to give, but to marry him herself. She cared about the business, about the people working there, and she especially cared about keeping her family safe.

He needed to make Sam see that he could offer her the security she needed; his name, his money, and his loyal friendship. To do that, he had to persuade her to accompany him on the cruise. Let her think it was for the purpose of finding him a wife. When she became aware of everything he had to offer, she would take it herself.

He pushed away the disquieting thought that she might want more, the love of which she had spoken, and undying passion. Those were the two things he was no longer prepared to give, no matter how much Jenny had insisted that he should. Nate clenched his jaw and moved with purpose up the front steps. Once on the porch, he shook loose the damp snow clinging to his boots, and pressed his finger to the bell.

The red nose of the Rudolph glued to the front door flashed on and off in the winter's night, blinding him with exuberant cheeriness. Strands of Christmas lights looped around the wide front porch, twinkling in waves like cheering fans at a football match.

An electrical hazard, Nate decided, peering at the place where the lights plugged into an extension cord.

A fire could spark there then travel the length of the frayed wiring and catch Santa's beard, which, judging from what he could see of the figure propped in the swing at the far end of the porch, appeared to have real hair.

Sam must have made the old gnome herself, stuffing a Santa suit with rags as you would a scarecrow in a field. He'd never seen anything like it, although he had to admit it looked good, as though Santa were a family friend resting on the porch awhile.

Turning back to the door, Nate stabbed the buzzer again. Still no one answered. He pressed his ear to the wood. *Jingle Bell Rock* trumpeted through the door, the sound of the music no doubt blanketing his ring. He gave a sharp knock, felt the release of some inner tension at the physical bashing of his knuckles against the wood.

Still no one. Irritated, he grabbed hold of the door handle, but before he could rattle it, the door jerked open.

A boy stood in the entrance and stared solemnly up at him through too-thick spectacles. 'Are you a burglar?' he asked.

'No,' Nate denied, releasing the handle.

'Then why were you opening our door?'

'No one came,' Nate explained.

'My mom says it's bad manners to just walk into people's houses.'

'Your mom's right.' Nate crouched down to where he could look the kid in the eye. 'Moms always are. Especially your mom.'

The boy smiled.

'Is she around?'

'Mom!' the boy hollered through the open door. 'Someone's here!' He turned back to Nate. 'What do you want her for?' he asked, his tone polite.

'I'm your mom's boss,' Nate said. 'I've got her Christmas present.'

The boy glanced at Nate's hands. 'I don't see any present.'

'It's in my pocket. I've got one for you too.'

'My mom told me never to take presents from strangers.'

'Good advice. You don't have to take it unless your mom says it's all right.'

'What is it?' the boy asked again.

'A cruise.'

'A cruise?'

'A ride on a big ship for ten days in the Caribbean.'

'I've seen boats like that on television.' The boy's eyes widened. 'They have swimming pools and video arcades?'

'They do.'

'And my mom would come too?'

'Yup.'

'And Grandma?'

'If she wants.'

'Wow! When?'

'Christmas Eve.'

'What about Santa?' The sparkle faded from the boy's eyes. 'He won't find us if we're not home on Christmas Eve.'

'Lots of people travel at Christmas. Santa always finds them.'

Sam's son's expression cleared. 'My mom's aunt came to visit two Christmases ago and Santa found her.'

'There you go.'

'So we can go!' The boy skipped up and down, then as suddenly as he'd moved, he doubled over in a fit of coughing.

'Whoa, young fella.' Nate awkwardly patted the boy on the back. 'That's some cold you've got there.' He rummaged in his pocket for the mint he'd received the night before with his dinner bill. When he found it, he handed it to Sam's son. 'We'll ask your mom if you can go. Ten days in the sun is just what you need.'

'But it's winter,' the child replied, unwrapping the mint and popping it into his mouth.

'Not in the Caribbean.'

Jamie grinned. 'I'll go get my mom.'

'Is your grandma here too?'

'She's in the living room. I'll get her if you want.'

'That would be great.' Nate held out his hand. 'By the way, my name's Nate. What's yours?'

'James Alexander Feldon,' the boy replied. He took hold of Nate's hand. 'But my friends call me Jamie.'

'Jamie,' Nate repeated. He stared down at the fingers engulfed by his own, felt the current flow between them as it had with the boy's mother. Only with Sam it had been electrical, the spark filling his veins with excitement and promise. This time the sensation was different, evoking in him the urge to protect, to safeguard this child with all the strength he possessed.

'Get your grandma,' he ordered, hastily dropping the child's hand.

Had he made a mistake?

He had thought it would be simple. Get Sam's boy and her grandmother excited about the trip, then Sam would have no reason to want to stay home. What mother could say no when her whole family said yes?

But spending time with Sam and her child could be dangerous. He needed to marry for the good of his business, and because it was what Jenny had wanted. But he couldn't get attached to his bride and her family. If he was smart, he would leave now and never come back.

'Can I help you?' a voice asked, as the Christmas rock jingle surged even louder.

Nate spun around. An oval-faced older woman stood in the doorway to the living room, looking curiously at him through blue eyes like Sam's. Only these eyes were faded while Sam's were intense.

Everything else about the woman was different; she was round where Sam was angular, had hair streaked white on grey while Sam's was blonde, and she had a mouth shaped like a rosebud while Sam's was wide and mobile.

'I've come to see Sam.' Nate held out his hand. 'I'm Nate Robbins.'

'So you're Nate!' the woman exclaimed. Her polite features melted into a smile that was just like Sam's, with the same generosity of expression and warmth of emotion.

'Guilty,' Nate replied. He fought again the urge to flee.

'I'm Ruby,' the woman said. 'Sam's grandmother.' She tucked her hand under his elbow. 'Come in and sit down,' she invited, leading him into the living room.

There weren't nearly as many Christmas lights inside the house as out, but in the corner, next to the fire, stood the most decorated tree Nate had ever laid eyes on.

Nothing matched. Not the lights, or the garlands, or the bells pulling down the ends of the branches. Strands of popcorn were strung everywhere, along with paper angels and aluminium foil stars. Nate picked up a square of aluminium foil. Hours must have been spent making the decorations, and from the look of the materials still scattered over the coffee table, they weren't finished yet.

Sam's grandmother glanced at the foil in Nate's hand. 'You'll have to make one, you know. My granddaughter will insist. I'll go get her,' Ruby offered.

'Jamie's getting her,' Nate said.

'It's nice of you to drop by.' Ruby gestured for him to sit on the overstuffed sofa.

'I've got a surprise for Sam.'

'What sort of surprise?'

'A sort of . . . Christmas present.'

'Oh?' Ruby said, sitting down next to him. 'What is it?'

'Sam has done a very good job since she joined the firm,' Nate said, not really answering. 'I don't know what I'd do without her.'

'She's not going anywhere,' her grandmother said, smiling.

'I know.' Nate frowned. 'But I've been worried about her lately.' As he spoke the words, Nate realized they were true. 'She's been working too hard — '

'She always has done.' A crease formed across Ruby's brow.

'She looks tired.'

'She is tired.' The old woman's eyes clouded. 'She is a single parent. She provides a home for me — '

'She told me what a help you are.'

'Help or not, having an extra mouth to feed is a strain.'

'She needs you,' Nate said firmly. 'She said you babysit Jamie. Seems like a nice kid.'

'Jamie's eight,' Ruby said proudly. 'He's a bit small for his age.'

'Sam's not very big.'

'Nor was her husband.' A frown creased Ruby's forehead.

'Where is her husband?' Nate asked.

'He took off the month after Jamie was born. Left Sam on her own to carry the load.'

His own parents had left him with Uncle Edward whenever they could, were busy with business, his uncle had always explained.

'Which is when I came to live with her,' Ruby went on. 'I take care of Jamie so Sam can work.'

And loved doing it, Nate could tell from the warmth in Ruby's eyes. To feel needed, to be part of a young family, was the best reason an older person had to stay alive. At least that's what Uncle Edward had always said.

'Doesn't Jamie's father help support him?'

'Doesn't even try,' Ruby said disgustedly. 'Probably knows my granddaughter would never accept anything from him.'

Nate's shoulders tensed. Another reason for marriage to be placed on a business-like footing. *He* wanted no risk of children, no possibility of causing pain. 'Why did they break up?'

'You'll have to ask Sam,' Ruby said. 'All I know is she hasn't trusted a man since.'

Nate crushed the foil he held in his hand, the anger surging through him jolting him with its intensity.

'Enough about ex-husbands.' Ruby glanced towards the door. 'Sam won't like it that I've told you about hers. She never talks about him.'

'She must be a strong woman to raise a child on her own.'

'Too strong for her own good! She should be out having fun. She's got me to babysit, but she shrugs me off whenever I suggest she go out on a date. Says she'd rather be home with us.'

'Fun is what I've got in mind,' Nate promised.

Ruby looked at him questioningly.

'My present.'

'Which is?'

'A ten-day Caribbean cruise,' Nate said heartily. The old lady had to like the idea. He needed her support to get Sam on board.

'By herself?' Ruby asked doubtfully.

'No,' Nate replied. 'I'll be there, and — '

'You're going!' The older woman's

glance was now approving. 'Sam didn't tell me the two of you were seeing each other.'

'It's nothing like — '

'Probably thought I'd disapprove.' Sam's grandmother shook her head, then stared hard at Nate. 'I like the look of you, young man, but you'll treat my granddaughter right or you'll answer to me.'

'Deal,' he said.

'Sam will never agree, of course,' Ruby said frankly. 'She won't want to leave me and Jamie. But don't worry. I'll work her around.'

'She won't have to leave anyone behind. You and Jamie are both invited.'

'You want *us* to go with you?'

'That's what I intended.'

'But you can't — '

'Sam needs this.' His fingers balled into his palm. 'I need her. It's not just her Christmas bonus. I have business on this cruise. I need Sam's help.'

'Business?' Ruby looked doubtful. 'It

won't be much of a holiday for Sam if she's working.'

'It's just a deal I have to put through before the end of the year. Don't worry, there'll be plenty of time left over for family. So,' he asked, 'what do you think?'

Ruby's face melted into a smile. 'When do we leave?'

'Christmas Eve,' Nate said. Relief coursed through him. 'Which only gives you a couple of days. But Sam could start her time off now so that if you have any shopping to do, like bathing suits or sun hats — '

The old woman's smile widened.

' — then she can take you to do it.'

'Take her to what?' a voice asked from the doorway to the hall.

Nate slowly stood and turned to face his assistant.

'What are you doing here?' Flour streaked Sam's face, but it failed to mask her stern expression. Jamie peeked out from behind his mother and shot him a grin.

'Really, Samantha,' her grandmother remonstrated. 'Is that any way to speak to a guest?'

'Depends on the guest.' Sam's gaze didn't waver from Nate's.

'I dropped by to wish you a Merry Christmas,' Nate explained.

'You did that at the office.'

'It can never be said too often.' He took the crushed foil he held in his hand and placed it onto a branch of the Christmas tree. It picked up the colours from the other ornaments and reflected them back in a cheerful illusion of movement.

'Pretty,' Sam said, stepping further into the room. Her apron was the type that looped around her neck, but the ties at the back hung loose, as though, when Jamie fetched her, she had just finished her baking. 'But what is it?'

'Whatever you want it to be.' Nate wrenched his gaze from Sam and glanced back at his creation. 'It seems to fit the tree's motif.'

'We do like a mix.' Sam's lips creased

into a smile. 'Jamie specializes in bells, Grams does the stars, and I do the angels.'

'Who did the birds, the little trees, and this — ' Nate peered towards the tree top, at a pointy object made of brown felt. ' — turkey?'

'It's a flying squirrel,' Sam replied indignantly. 'Which I made, I'll have you know.' Then she frowned again at him. 'But you haven't answered my question. What are you doing here?'

'He's brought presents, Mom,' Jamie said excitedly. Hopping on one foot, he flung himself between them.

Sam's frown deepened. 'What sort of presents?'

'A trip on a big ship.' The boy leaned back against his mother and gazed expectantly up at Nate.

'Mr. Robbins has made a mistake.' Sam glared at Nate over the top of Jamie's head. 'I've already told him I can't go on any trip.' She brandished the mixing spoon she still clutched in one hand and flour dribbled onto the floor. 'It's Christmas. My place is here.' She glanced at her son. 'With Jamie and Grams.'

'We're all going!' her son cried.

'We can't go. It's Christmas.'

'But he's got the tickets,' the boy protested.

'Tickets!' Sam glanced back at Nate, her eyes glinting dangerously. 'You've got tickets?'

'Your Christmas bonus,' Nate explained.

'There is no bonus.'

'Warm air,' he went on hastily, 'sea breezes, tropical fish, lounging around outside in the sun all day. It'll be just the thing to get rid of Jamie's cold.'

As if on cue, the boy coughed.

'Think about it, Sam,' Nate encouraged his assistant softly. 'It'll be fun.'

'We'll have fun here. We never go away at Christmas. We've got the tree, done the baking. Nobody wants to give that up.'

'Ask them,' he suggested.

'I want to go,' Jamie cried excitedly. 'Nate said — '

'Mr. Robbins,' his mother corrected.

' — that there'll be swimming pools, and arcade games, and snorkelling, and — '

'What about our tree?' his mother asked. 'And our Christmas dinner, and Santa Claus — '

'Nate says Santa will find us wherever we go.'

'Nate says,' Sam repeated, casting Nate an icy look.

'I understand they play bingo on board these ships,' Ruby murmured.

'Bingo, blackjack, slots — '

'I never gamble,' the old woman said primly. 'I just play a little bingo now and then.'

'They have bingo,' Nate promised. 'Every day. Maybe twice a day!'

'Grams!' Sam protested.

'It's a very generous offer,' her grandmother chided. 'I think you should accept.'

'Generous!' Sam cried. 'It's not

generous at all. He just wants me to come so that I'll — ' She covered Jamie's ears. 'I don't want to tell you what he wants me to do.'

'Whatever it is, you'd better do it,' her grandmother advised.

Nate smiled at Ruby then ducked as Sam's mixing spoon sailed towards him. The spoon hit the tree behind him, settling into its branches like an oversize bird.

'Bed,' Sam told Jamie, her cheeks brilliant red. She pulled her protesting son in the direction of the door. 'And you,' she ordered Nate, in a voice that shook, 'you stay where you are. I'll be back in a minute.'

# 3

Sam glowered at the envelope of tickets on her dashboard. Three tickets for two rooms. One for her, and one for Jamie and her grandmother. Both outside cabins, amidships.

Awesome, Jamie had said.

Generous, her grandmother had added.

Manipulative, Sam had silently cursed. What infuriated her the most was that a tiny part of her longed to go on this trip, to do something she'd never done before, to live a little before she died of apoplexy! Which was what was likely to happen the way Nate Robbins riled her up.

How dare the man! She'd told him in his office how she felt about the trip, but he'd bought the tickets anyway, had somehow persuaded her family to want to go. Then instead of waiting to talk it through as she had instructed, he'd handed the tickets to her grandmother and taken off.

Well, he wasn't getting away with it.

Sam pounded on the steering wheel of her Datsun, wincing as her frozen fingers met the unrelenting metal. She held them to her lips and blew, praying her breath's warmth would melt away the stiffness.

There hadn't been such a cold December in Seattle in over ten years. It was time she found the money from somewhere to get the car's heater fixed. Sighing deeply, she blew on her fingers again.

Some tropical warmth would feel good on her cold skin, as would swaying in a hammock on a tropical beach. She could almost taste the explosion of fruit punch and rum after sipping a cool drink through a long plastic straw.

With a rapid shake of her head, Sam thrust her fantasies from her mind and curled her frozen fingers into her palms.

She had to stick to her guns about this trip, couldn't afford to change her mind for the sake of creature comforts. Ten days in paradise meant ten days close to Nate, and the attraction she already felt for him could only lead to heartache.

Nate was intent on marrying a woman he didn't love, and she wanted a man who would love her for ever.

The traffic light turned green and Sam pressed her foot to the accelerator. She had to get this over, had to tell Nate what she thought of his behaviour and throw his tickets back in his face.

★ ★ ★

Easier said than done, she realized, the minute Nate opened the door to his condominium. It was hard to stay angry when he looked at her as though, despite their many differences, he was delighted to see her.

'I told you to wait,' she said, frowning. She pushed past him into his living room. 'I wanted to talk to you.'

'You seemed busy,' Nate said.

Her pulse pounded against her temples, shafting a pain through her head.

'Sit down,' he went on, gesturing towards the couch.

There was a pillow at one end that still held the shape of his head, while a half-empty wine glass rested on the coffee table next to it. From the notes of the alto sax spiralling from the stereo, he'd been lying in the semi-darkness listening to some blues.

Not very Christmassy.

Sympathy tugged at her heart. With a fierce effort, she squelched it and cast a glance around the rest of the room. No tree, no lights, not even a box of chocolates.

'Care for a drink?' Nate asked.

'I can't stay,' she replied. She intended only to give him a piece of her mind then leave before he could convince her to go on a world cruise! With a shiver, she tucked her scarf more tightly around her neck and wondered if Nate's house was truly as cold as her car, or if it was the lack of decor that was freezing her soul.

'I haven't settled in yet,' Nate explained, as though he had managed to read her mind.

'How long have you lived here?'

'Two years last June.'

'Two and a half years!' she exclaimed. 'Where's all your stuff?'

'I don't have any stuff.'

'Everyone has stuff!' She certainly had. Her own clutter at times got the best of her and when it did she launched into a cleaning blitz. But as she had often explained to her friend Cheryl, who lived in as tidy an environment as three young daughters allowed, at least her clutter had life. 'You have no pictures,' she accused, 'no books — '

'I have pictures,' Nate protested. Then his face closed over as though he wished he'd said nothing.

'Where?' she demanded.

'I'll get you that drink now,' he replied, and before she could ask again, he moved towards the kitchen.

Perhaps a drink was what she needed after the day she'd just had. Perhaps with drinks in hand, they could discuss this cruise business in a civilized fashion.

'White wine,' she called after him.

'Make yourself at home,' he answered, disappearing through a door.

Home was not a word she'd use to describe this place, where the only easy chair was stacked high with office papers. She followed Nate instead, noting as she went that while his furniture was of good quality, nothing about it gave out warmth. It was all leather and metal, with cold bits of glass.

'Want something to eat?' Nate asked, as she entered the kitchen, his voice muffled by the open door of the fridge.

'I didn't come here to eat.'

'We can't talk on an empty stomach.'

He stretched forward and pulled another wine bottle from the back. 'Chardonnay?'

'Anything.'

He poured her a glass, then turned back to continue his perusal of the fridge's contents. 'How about Chinese?' he finally said, pulling out a bowl of something covered in a greyish fuzz.

'Order in, you mean?' she asked.

'Unless you want to risk these leftovers.'

'They look as though they've been there for months.' Sam shuddered. There was no way they could eat the contents of the bowl, but she didn't want to order in either. It would take too much time, and she was already staying too long in the company of this man.

'Not months,' Nate replied, dropping the bowl and its contents into the garbage. 'But I do have wine!'

'You can't live on wine.'

'I eat out a lot.'

'It's Christmas.' She eyed him

sternly. 'Haven't you done your food shopping yet?'

'I'm going away, remember. No sense cluttering up the fridge with food I won't eat.'

'You only decided this morning that you were going away.'

'If I hadn't booked the cruise I would have gone to Uncle Edward's, and made sure everything was all right with Mrs. Mulroy and Samson.'

'What about your family?' She'd never heard him talk of parents, or siblings, or anything else that a family entailed. She told herself curiosity forced the question from her, not caring or a deepening interest in her boss.

'Mrs. Mulroy and Samson are my family.' The familiar forbidding glint reappeared in her boss's eyes. 'What would you like? Chinese or pizza? Or we could go out.'

'No,' she replied hastily. That would be worse than ordering in. It would seem like a date. 'Move aside,' she ordered, edging past him to look into the fridge herself. 'You must have something in here besides rotting takeaway and booze.'

'I've got eggs, I think.'

'You do,' she affirmed. She reached past a plastic bag of wrinkled grapes to grab hold of the carton. She sought the date on the side of the box. 'Still good,' she pronounced, flashing him a swift smile. 'And here's some cheddar and a tomato. What are *you* doing with a tomato?'

'I can cook,' he said indignantly.

She laughed.

'But if you're afraid, you can do the cooking.'

'If you do the dishes, you've got yourself a deal.'

With a smile he poured out two glasses of wine then clicked the rim of her glass with his.

★　★　★

'So?' she asked, scrutinizing his face.

'Delicious,' he pronounced. He

scooped up the last of his omelette with the French bread Sam had found buried under pizza in the freezer.

She couldn't stop a smile from widening her lips. Nate Robbins might want everything his own way, and might not be able to cook, but he'd made her efforts feel a pleasure. He had leaned against the counter while she beat eggs and grated cheese and commented with dry humour that when he'd tried to do the same, he'd nearly sliced off his finger.

He had set the table, however, had even unearthed a pair of candlesticks from a cupboard below the sink and thrust into them a pair of candles some six inches different in length. When he'd lowered the kitchen lights with a theatrical flourish, the effect had been magical.

It felt good cooking for a man again, especially a man like Nate whose appreciation showed in his eyes.

A man who wanted to marry the nearest available woman, Sam

reminded herself sternly, whether he loved her or not.

'Time to talk,' she said, her good humour dissipating.

'Dishes first,' Nate said firmly. He rose to his feet.

She stood also and placed her hand on Nate's. She had intended to simply stop him, to make him talk, but the same thing happened as when they'd touched in the office, only this time the electricity between them was stronger.

'Leave the dishes,' she insisted, snatching her hand away.

'What about your passports?' he asked. 'Are they in order?'

'I didn't come here to talk about passports!'

'You're right. We might not need them. I'll ask the travel agent.'

'Nate!' she said threateningly.

'What?' he asked. He leaned against the counter and crossed his arms over his chest. 'What do you want to talk about?'

'The trip,' she said firmly. 'You

manipulated my family and me.'

'Manipulated you!' One black brow lifted. 'I asked if you'd like to come and you told me you couldn't. When I asked you why, you told me you didn't want to leave your family. I realized that of course you couldn't go away at Christmas without them, but I thought if they wanted to go, then you'd be happy about going yourself.'

'Well, I'm not.'

'Why not? Your family is.'

'They wouldn't be if you hadn't asked them behind my back.'

'You do realize,' Nate said, 'how ridiculous that sounds?'

Sam gritted her teeth. 'It's not ridiculous. You did go behind my back.'

'But you'll come?'

'Are you asking *me* now?'

'I asked you before.' He took a step closer. 'Now I'm asking you again.'

He was standing so near she could smell his scent, like a sea breeze after the rain, mixed with candles, and wine, and the earthy smell of garlic.

'It'll be fun Sam,' he urged. 'You need a little fun.'

'I have fun,' she protested. 'Jamie and I play games. We have friends over for dinner.' It wasn't the sort of fun a cruise ship offered, the sort of fun she would never have if she had to pay for it herself. It took all her resources just to keep her family on firm ground.

'Even your grandmother says you need fun,' Nate went on.

'My grandmother says too much.'

'So we're agreed?' Nate asked, in a business-like tone. 'You'll all come?'

For an instant, she hesitated, wanting to hold strong, then with a rush of excitement, breathlessly said, 'Yes.'

'Wonderful!' Nate replied.

Before she could protest, before she could even think, he pulled her into his arms and kissed her.

It seemed to Sam that all time stood still, and it felt as though it would never begin again. His lips, at first, were the lips of a friend, lightly grazing hers with a friend's sort of kiss. Then his mouth

60

hardened and explored the curve of hers.

Her eyes, which she had closed, fluttered open once more, and when she looked into his eyes, she saw desire. It overwhelmed her, confused her, and just when she decided she didn't want to deny it, wanted to kiss him back with all the ardour he had thrust at her, he stiffened and pulled away.

'I'm sorry,' he said, his breath still sweet on her face.

'I — '

'Don't say anything,' he ordered. 'That kiss shouldn't have happened.'

'It doesn't matter,' Sam whispered. Desperately, she tried to still the pounding of her heart. 'It's the wine, the day — ' She licked her suddenly dry lips. ' — it's been quite a day.'

'Yes.' Then his eyelids hooded and all expression was blocked.

She took a step backwards. 'I agreed to go on the cruise. If you want me I still will.'

'Good,' he replied, but appeared

suddenly a stranger.

'Which way to your washroom?' She had to get away, had to throw cold water on her hot face and figure out what had just happened.

'Through the living-room,' he replied, 'and down the hall to your right.'

She bolted through the door, but once out of sight, slowed and leaned against the wall. Pressing her fingers to her lips, she could still feel Nate's heat. She had promised to help him, to go with him on the cruise, but how could she keep that promise after kissing him like that and being kissed in return? How could she be near him for the next ten days?

Because she had to, she decided, tightening her jaw, for Jamie, for her grandmother, but most of all for herself. She had to put this attraction for Nate Robbins into its proper place. Once he was married, he'd be out of reach.

With a sigh, she glanced at the

glass-topped table to her left. Nate had told the truth. He did have pictures. Three of them sat right there on the table. Somehow she had missed them when she passed by the first time.

She picked up the closest one, felt the warmth of the wooden frame, saw a young Nate with the same piercing eyes the older Nate possessed. The grey-haired man next to him must be his great-uncle Edward. The two were smiling at each other, looking happy and content.

Sam slowly placed the picture back and picked up the next one. A wedding photo this time of a younger Nate and an unknown dark-haired woman, whose eyes shone with joy as she gazed at her husband.

Pain pierced Sam's chest. Nate had never said he had been married. Nor had anyone at work ever mentioned he'd had a wife.

With a trembling hand, she put the photo down. Slowly, carefully, she picked up the next. Pain drove to her gut and a cry flew to her lips, but she stifled the sound by thrusting her hand to her mouth.

Nate's wife was in this picture also, but she stood alone in a grass-filled pasture. Standing sideways to the camera, her hands gently caressed her rounded belly.

She was pregnant. With a baby. Nate's baby.

The room began to spin. Sam pressed her palms against the wall and forced her world to stillness. Slowly, stiffly, she made her way to the sofa, but once collapsed upon it, the image of Nate's wife still swirled in her brain, looking as she had looked in the photo on the table, filled with joy and new life.

A wife Nate had never mentioned. Had Nate, like Phil, left his family?

'Are you all right?' Nate's voice suddenly demanded.

She turned to face him. 'Why didn't you tell me?'

'Tell you what?'

'That you're already married.' Her

throat felt so tight she thought it might crack.

He glanced sharply toward the table holding the pictures. 'I'm not married,' he growled. 'Not anymore.'

Sam gathered her strength and stood. 'You're just like all the rest, men who find it so easy to leave.'

'You don't know — '

'I do know. So does my son.' She swallowed hard. 'I didn't think you were like that.'

'I'm not.'

'Would your wife agree? Or your child?'

His face turned so white it became the face of a ghost. 'My wife's dead,' he said, 'and so is my daughter.'

'Dead?' All heat fled Sam's body.

'Five years ago.'

'Why didn't you — ?' She tried to finish the questions, but the words wouldn't come and when she tried to move towards him, her legs wouldn't go.

'It doesn't matter.' He shook his

head. 'Nothing matters.'

'If you'd rather get someone else to help on the cruise — '

'I don't want anyone else.' He took hold of her arm in a grip so tight, all circulation died. 'Why don't *you* just marry me, Sam, and we'll be done with this business?'

# 4

Thank God, when he had asked, she had told him no, for when he'd first asked, he hadn't really known her, and when he asked again, it was in a moment of insane reaction to the evening they had just spent together, laughing and talking and enjoying each other's company. The sort of evening he hadn't experienced with a woman since Jenny died, the sort of evening he had no intention of ever experiencing again.

He couldn't afford to marry a woman whose vision of marriage included undying love and lasting commitment. It was something Sam deserved, something she should have, but it wasn't for him. Not anymore. Not when the last time he'd tried it, his world had fallen apart.

Nate shrugged his briefcase to his other hand and tried to keep his gaze averted from the sight of Sam's legs twinkling up the gangplank in front of him. But their shapely form enticed, drawing the attention of every male within viewing distance as they extended gracefully from beneath the hem of her sea-blue sundress. The same blue as her eyes, Nate decided, scowling.

Suddenly Sam paused and turned to face him as the line of passengers in front of her halted. Her gaze met his in a laser-sharp piercing of heat and light.

'Is your bag too heavy?' she asked.

'No,' he growled. For the thousandth time, he wished the trip was over, for by then, married or not, he'd at least be done with the effort of trying.

'Then stop looking as though you're being tortured,' she ordered. 'This is a cruise ship, not life imprisonment. If you're going to attract the attention of eligible women, you have to learn to smile.'

'Like this?' he asked, adjusting his

lips into an upward curve.

'Better,' she said, laughing.

'So you're talking to me again, then?' Sam's silence had been deafening on the flight from Seattle to Fort Lauderdale.

'I was never not talking to you.'

'Good,' he said, 'because we have to talk about what happened the other night.'

Her eyes darkened. 'Nothing happened.'

'I don't want you to be uncomfortable.' He suddenly felt as though he were in his office still, as though he was wearing his business shirt and its collar was choking him.

'I'm not uncomfortable.' Her gaze flickered sideways.

'You're lying.'

'Nothing happened. I don't want to talk about it.' She gestured meaningfully toward her son ahead of her on the ramp. 'Especially not here.' She took hold of Jamie's hand.

'Aw, Mom,' the boy protested. The

teddy bear he held nearly tumbled into the ocean.

'Later then,' Nate insisted. Somehow they had to lay the incident to rest, no matter how uncomfortable it made them feel. It seemed the only way to put this woman from his mind.

The line began to move again, but the quilt Jamie was holding in his other hand suddenly fell, blanketing the boy's feet in a tangle of dinosaur shapes and colours. Nate reached past Sam and grabbed hold of both the quilt and Jamie, steadying the child and folding the quilt over his own arm.

His mother had made the quilt, Jamie had told Nate on the plane, leaning across the aisle separating them as though intent on his mother not hearing.

He didn't need a *blankie* anymore, the boy had added in a whisper, but he hadn't liked to leave it behind. A furrow creased the boy's forehead. If he didn't bring it along, the dinosaurs might get lonely, and if that happened there was

70

no telling what they might do. They might even start eating one another!

Grinning at the memory, Nate's spirits unexpectedly lightened. From the plethora of bags hanging off Jamie's arms and shoulders, and the second teddy poking its head through the zipper of his backpack, it was obvious the quilt wasn't the only item Sam's son had been reluctant to leave behind. The kid must have brought along every toy he owned.

Sam hadn't packed any lighter. Her belongings had filled three suitcases and a duffle bag!

Nate didn't even want to think about what Ruby had brought. The old woman had insisted he pull out a battered trunk from the far corner of Sam's attic, a receptacle looking as old as Civil War times.

A sea trunk, Ruby had pronounced, with a satisfied expression, as they all stood sneezing from the trunk top's dust. The one her grandfather had used when he emigrated from England. Sam had declared worriedly that the trunk would never fit in the back of her Volkswagen, and it was then Nate had offered to pick them all up and take them to the airport himself.

At least the bustle and confusion had blanketed the awkwardness between him and Sam, an awkwardness Nate wished he could simply erase. If they'd dealt with the situation that night, not allowed it to grow and fester, then they wouldn't have to have the conversation he knew they needed.

Gritting his teeth, Nate wished all women in general and Sam Feldon in particular, a swift trip to hell and back.

* * *

'Our cabins are all in a row,' Jamie said excitedly, reading off the numbers and running through the door of the last in line. 'Look, Grandma, this one's ours!' He edged past their checked luggage which had been deposited in front of their door, and flung himself onto the nearest bed.

'Take the one nearest the window, dear,' Ruby replied. 'I want the bed closest to the bathroom.' She winked at Nate and Sam as the boy scooted to lay his bag on top of his bed.

'Are you sure you don't want my room, Grams?' Sam asked worriedly, watching as her son tipped his stuffed animals from his knapsack and lined them up along the windowsill. 'You're going to be exhausted enough dealing with Jamie when I have to work without having to sleep with him as well.'

'Jamie and I will be fine. Besides — ' She glanced past Sam to where Nate stood in the doorway. ' — you're bound to be up late most nights — dancing, or whatever.'

'I wouldn't count on it,' Sam muttered, cursing the heat sweeping her cheeks.

'You'll both be out dancing,' Nate said with a smile. 'The travel agent assured me there are plenty of babysitters on board should we need one.'

'There you are then,' Ruby said. 'It's all settled. I'll stay with Jamie, Sam, and you take the room next door. Now, Nate, if you could just push my trunk into the room and set it next to this cupboard, I'll unpack.'

Sam stepped to one side as Nate heaved the trunk past her then moved swiftly to her own room. It was just like Jamie and Ruby's, only in hers, the bed was king-size. The heat on Sam's cheeks blazed hotter. She'd been too busy taking care of Jamie these last few years to need a bed this size.

Maybe things could change. Maybe on this cruise she'd meet a man who desired the same things as she, a man with whom she could share her life.

'Looks good,' Nate said, the sound of his voice startling her.

She spun around. 'What does?'

'The view of the harbour.' He glanced past her to the bed.

'Don't even think — '

'Just practising. You told me to smile, to flirt — '

'You said you'd forgotten how.'

He lifted one brow. 'Meet me on the Lido deck in ten minutes,' he said. 'We'll have a drink and raise a toast to the success of this voyage.'

Which for Nate meant marriage, Sam thought, suddenly dismal. She watched as his back disappeared through her door. Marriage without love.

★   ★   ★

The Lido deck was huge. No matter which direction Sam looked, all she saw were people. All of whom appeared to know exactly what they were supposed to be doing, and all of whom looked to be having fun.

She tweaked the hemline of her new dress straight and edged through the crowd to the rail. Nate could find her if he wanted to talk that badly. Until he did, she was going to order one of the tall drinks everyone was holding and stand by the rail and wave farewell to land.

Only the boat wasn't moving.

She peered down the ship's side and saw bags still being trundled across a gangplank on one of the lower levels.

'Samantha? Samantha Birk?'

'Sam Feldon,' Sam corrected, turning and peering through the crowd behind her. Feldon was her maiden name. She had reverted to using it when her divorce had become final.

'And here's me thinking I was clever to remember your married name,' a woman replied, her face suddenly visible as the cluster of people around Sam parted.

'Fay?' Sam said incredulously. 'Fay Parkinson?'

'Guilty. Although it's Miller now.' Fay pushed her sunglasses off her nose and onto her head, raking back her auburn hair as she did so. 'My God, how long has it been? Seven years? Eight?'

'About eight,' Sam said, suddenly remembering the last time she'd seen

Fay. She and Phil had been walking in front of Pike's Market, no doubt appearing to strangers as a happy young couple out for the day with their new baby.

Only they hadn't been happy. Phil was already complaining that he'd envisioned a life of parties and travel, not one filled with babies in diapers and mortgages he couldn't afford.

'So where's . . . Rick, wasn't it?'

'Phil.' Sam glanced down and frowned at the cherry floating in her drink. Incredible how swiftly the time had passed since she'd first known Fay, although knowing her was not an entirely accurate description of their relationship. She wasn't sure they'd even spoken in all their years of high school, for the woman opposite had moved in a different crowd, a glamorous crowd made up of boys in sleek cars and girls in expensive clothes.

'I don't know where Phil is,' Sam continued, dragging her attention back to Fay. 'We're divorced.' At least she was able now, after eight years of practise, to say the word as though it meant nothing.

Fay laughed. 'Who isn't? I've just finished with number two myself.' Her eyes narrowed. 'But you had a child, didn't you? What happened to him?'

'I have Jamie.'

'Well, that's good.' She grimaced. 'At least, I suppose it is.'

'Very good,' Sam said firmly. 'What about you? Any kids?'

'Never!' Fay shuddered. 'Deadly to one's social life.'

'Not something I have to worry about,' Sam said, smiling, feeling the familiar gladness that she had her son instead.

'You'll soon change that,' Fay decreed. 'That's what cruises are for, after all.'

'Romance . . . adventure?' Sam suggested.

'Exactly.'

'Well, I'm here to work.'

'Work?' Fay's eyebrows lifted. 'You

work for the cruise company?' She swept a dubious glance over Sam's new dress.

A dress on which she'd spent far too much of last month's salary, but even with that, it wasn't what a woman like Fay would call glamorous, or match the styles she'd already seen on board the ship.

'What's your job?' Fay went on. 'Cruise director?' This last question was uttered even more doubtfully than the first, as though Fay thought her no more capable of being a cruise director than Homecoming Queen.

'No.' Sam stifled a giggle. 'Although that would be a great job for someone without kids.'

'Not for me, darling.' Fay firmly placed her glasses once more over her eyes. 'I'm on this cruise for fun, not to amuse old biddies from the midwest.'

'Somehow,' Sam said dryly, thinking of her grandmother, 'I think the midwest biddies know more about fun than we'll ever know.'

'Each to their own.' Fay's gaze slid off Sam and scanned the crowd, as though bored with this talk of old women's amusements. 'Let's find a couple of deck chairs and get another drink. We've got some serious catching up to do.'

'Well, I — ' Sam scanned the passengers milling around. 'I have to meet someone.'

'Already! You work fast.'

'No, I didn't mean — '

'Let him find you.' Fay took hold of Sam's elbow and pushed a path through the throngs six deep at the railing. 'Men appreciate a woman who doesn't make herself too available.'

'I didn't say it was a man.'

'Well, isn't it?' Fay asked, shooting her a shrewd glance.

'Not in the way you mean.'

'What other way is there?'

'Not every man is a target.'

'That's where you're wrong.' Fay shook her mane of auburn hair off her shoulders. 'All men are susceptible to the spell of a beautiful woman. And you've turned out rather attractive. Who would have thought?'

'My mother for one,' Sam muttered, annoyed that a decade-old opinion from a high school acquaintance still had the power to make her cross.

'Mothers don't count,' Fay said dismissively. 'My mother still thinks I should have married Billy Winston.'

'Why didn't you?' Sam asked. 'You went together for ages.'

'No prospects, darling. He was a lot of fun, but fun doesn't pay the bills. And trust me — ' Her amber eyes sobered. ' — *that* takes serious money.'

'You always looked as though you were in love.'

'Anyone can fall in love.'

'Weren't you voted the couple most likely to get married?'

Fay ducked past a leather-skinned geriatric and his plump wife and placed her purse on a plastic table set between two deck chairs. 'What do teenagers know?' she asked, gracefully settling herself into the chair on the right.

'Everything,' Sam replied, wiggling contentedly against the other chair's padded cushion, 'or so we thought.'

'I thought you planned to go back east to college?' Fay raised her hand and snagged a drink off a passing steward.

'That was the plan, but — '

'You fell in love,' Fay guessed.

'Yes.'

'And out of it again?'

'Something like that.' She didn't want to discuss her marriage, especially with this woman she barely knew.

'I'm not saying divorce doesn't hurt,' Fay continued.

Sam glanced at her swiftly, was stunned to find sympathy in the other woman's eyes.

'But you have to get over it,' Fay said firmly. 'Next time take marriage with a grain of salt.'

'What do you mean?'

'People marry each other for all sorts

of reasons. For companionship — '

'Even my grandmother wouldn't marry for companionship,' Sam protested, 'and she's seventy-five!'

' — for business — '

'Business!'

'Businessmen often don't want the work of a wife and children. They simply want someone to make their lives easier, someone who'll arrange their social life but make no demands on a personal level, who'll look good on their arm but don't need wooing, who'll — '

'I don't believe — '

'Believe it. More people than you think marry because it's a mutually beneficial situation. Don't get duped into thinking love is all that matters.'

'It is!'

'It ends,' Fay said definitely. 'Sooner or later, it always ends.'

'Why did you marry if you believe all you're saying?'

'Money, darling — ' Fay raised her drink to her lips and took a long sip.

' — the most powerful aphrodisiac of them all.'

'I should introduce you to my boss.'

'Your boss?' Fay asked. 'Why?'

'He wants to get married.'

'What's he like?' Fay's gaze suddenly focussed intently on Sam's.

'Well . . . ' Why had she even mentioned Nate, or said that he wished to marry? Despite her boss's present crazy plan, he was really a great guy, and deserved more out of life than marriage to a woman like Fay.

'What's he like?' Fay asked again.

'Just your average guy.' Sam shrugged. 'Nothing special.' But special was a word that fit Nate like a glove. And it was because of his specialness that she cared so much. The thought of him wasting his life on a woman he didn't love filled her with horror.

Not that she had any personal interest in that direction herself. It was just that after two years of working with him, she felt that she knew him, had liked him from the first day they met, even thought of him as a friend despite her efforts to think of him only as her employer.

'Average.' Fay grimaced. 'Best to stay away from average, darling. There's nothing in average for women like you and me.'

'I'm not sure we're that alike.'

Amusement laced Fay's eyes. 'We're not at all alike. But you have potential — ' Again, she looked Sam over from her head to her toes. ' — definitely potential.'

'Potential for what?' For the second time that day Sam was glad she was no longer in high school, no longer dependant on the opinion of in-crowders for personal validation.

'You've got a certain look.' Fay examined her face. 'Not prettiness exactly. More good skin, classical features . . . and your hair is wonderful! What colour does your hairdresser use?'

'It's natural,' Sam said dryly. Her hair was the one feature on which she could always count.

'If you say so,' Fay said doubtfully.

'Trust me.'

'Whatever.' Her classmate's eyes narrowed. 'But you still haven't said why you're working while on vacation.'

'It's . . . private.'

'Hm.' The other woman cast her a knowing smile.

'What do you mean?'

Fay shrugged. 'A cruise ship, vacation time, here alone with your boss . . . sounds nice.'

'What are you saying?'

'You wouldn't be the first couple to take a vacation together and call it business.'

'We're not a couple!' Heat swept Sam's cheeks. 'And it is business.' Though not the sort they normally conducted, or the sort in which she even wanted to be involved.

'Sam.'

Sam turned at the unmistakable sound of Nate's voice.

'Here you are,' he said.

'Your boss?' Fay hissed softly.

Wordlessly, Sam nodded.

'Average?' Fay murmured. Her tone indicated clearly she would no longer believe a word Sam said.

Anything but average, Sam decided miserably. Nate's dark hair was ruffled by the off-shore breeze, and his skin seemed already tanned against his open-necked cotton shirt. He looked as natural on board this ship as he did in the office, as though he'd been born to the heat of the tropics and the luxury of the liner.

'I've been looking for you.' Nate halted in front of Sam.

'I told her you would.' Fay languidly held out her hand.

'Nate, this is Fay,' Sam said reluctantly, 'an old classmate from high school.'

'Not so old,' Fay contradicted, smiling her old smile, the one that in high school had stopped the boys dead.

Men, too, Sam realised dismally, noting the sudden appreciation gleaming in Nate's eyes.

'Fay Miller,' Fay elaborated. 'And your last name is . . . ?'

'Robbins.' Nate took Fay's hand, seemed to hold it too long.

'Sam's boss,' Fay added, a smile curving her lips.

Nate glanced at Sam, a question in his eyes.

'I was just explaining to Fay that we're on a business trip,' she said.

'That's right,' Nate agreed, 'though there'll be plenty of time for pleasure.'

Fay turned to Sam, her eyebrows lifting.

'We're ironing out some problems that cropped up at work,' Sam explained hastily. Heat burned her cheeks.

'Call it business if you like,' Fay said with a laugh, 'but you don't have to pussyfoot around me.'

'My son and grandmother are with me,' Sam hastened on.

'Good cover,' Fay said approvingly, 'though hardly necessary in this day and age.'

'You're right,' Sam said. 'They do tend to cramp one's style.' Nate looked startled when she said that, but if he was going to drop her in it with Fay, he could darn well share the consequences. 'But I couldn't leave them at home for Christmas,' she added sweetly.

'Of course not,' Fay agreed. She turned her attention back to Nate. 'I take it you like children?'

He didn't answer.

'Oh well, with Sam's grandmother along, at least you've got a babysitter.'

Which was exactly what Nate had said. Although he had made the comment unthinkingly, and when the time had actually come to depart, had enthusiastically listed on the way to the airport, all the activities available to Ruby on board ship.

'If you'll excuse us, Fay,' Nate said politely, 'I need to steal Sam away for a moment.'

'Of course.' Fay crossed her shapely legs with eye-catching slowness. 'Don't do anything I wouldn't do.'

# 5

'There's nothing she wouldn't do,' Sam murmured beneath her breath.

Nate unceremoniously took hold of her elbow and tugged her along the deck.

'Let go,' she added, shaking off his hand.

'Did you tell her why we're here?' Nate demanded.

'Did it sound as though I told her?' Sam's cheeks blazed hot.

'Yes,' he snapped. 'All that innuendo, that banter — '

'It's called flirting. Get used to it.'

'I know what it's called!'

'You told me in Seattle that you didn't!'

'I said I'd forgotten how to do it, not that I couldn't recognize it.' He glowered at her. 'What exactly did you tell her?'

'Just that we're here on business,' Sam lied. 'It was *you* who told her we were here for pleasure. People will get the wrong idea if you go around saying things like that.'

'The wrong idea?'

'That we're here on some sort of assignation.' She placed her hands on her hips. 'Which will ruin any plans you might have of getting to know other women.'

'I don't see how — '

'Don't see how? If you're dating me, that's as good as slapping a hands-off sign on your backside.'

'Fay didn't seem to be taking much notice of any sign.'

'Fay's Fay. She's not your garden variety female.'

'I noticed.' His lips twitched.

'So why on earth did you say we were on this trip for pleasure?'

'Didn't like to lie.'

'You're going to have to lie if you intend to find a wife within a week.'

'I don't see why.'

'Because whether you believe in romance or not, no woman wants to think she's being asked to marry a man simply to enable her husband to inherit a fortune.'

'It's as good a reason as any.'

'It's humiliating!'

'Is that why you said no?'

If he could have pulled the question back, he'd have done so in an instant. He'd been relieved before when she'd allowed the notion to drop without discussion. Now, as though the devil himself resided within, he'd brought up the issue for a second time.

He could hardly bear to look at her, to see her arms drop from her hips, and her face lose its colour, to see the stuffing flow out as from a rip in a Raggedy Ann.

'You know why I said no.' Sam's words emerged tersely.

'Forget it then.'

'I thought we had.'

She stared at him as though there were only the two of them on this ship, as though all nineteen hundred passengers had disembarked and left them to sail the tropical seas alone. For the sounds of excited laughter and the babble of tongues had disappeared, and in its wake there was only silence.

Nate took a deep breath. 'Why do I have to lie?'

'I didn't mean you had to lie.' Sam's eyes signalled her gratitude that he'd dropped the question of marriage. 'I just meant you have to approach this in a more traditional manner.'

'If I have to promise to love, honour and obey, I can't do it at all.' When he had married Jenny, he had said those words and had meant them with all his heart, would have died to protect their meaning.

'I'm not saying you have to promise anything,' Sam said softly, 'but women want more than money and status when they enter into marriage.'

'That's all that's on offer. Besides, look around you. You surely don't believe all these couples are joined by the bonds of love.'

'I think they were when they began,' Sam said, in a voice so low, Nate could scarcely hear her. 'But that's not the point. You only have seven days.'

'Long enough,' he said. It had taken him only seven hours to fall in love with Jenny. He didn't want that this time, didn't want to care so much his heart would rip again from his chest when inevitably everything turned out wrong.

'Not if it's a business merger,' Sam countered. 'Which is what you have in mind. That could take weeks. You'd need attorneys with pre-nups, and contracts and guarantees — '

'Guarantees of what?'

'Of whatever it is you're offering for the privilege of becoming your wife.'

'You make it sound impossible.'

'It is. That's what I've been saying.'

'I thought you were here to help.'

'I am.' She sighed. 'But we have to come up with a game plan that will work.'

He felt enough of a cheat already.

Uncle Edward's insistence on the conditions of his will being met hadn't intended this netherworld of pain and reluctance.

Nate had thought he had a game plan, could achieve his goal without lying, was offering something many woman would jump at.

Sam's forehead creased. 'I don't mean you have to lie exactly.'

'What then?'

'Just do what men do when they meet someone they like. Smile a lot. Be attentive, amusing — '

'Amusing!'

'You can be amusing.' She flashed him a smile. 'You've made me laugh often enough.'

'So where does the lying come in?'

'Don't tell them why you want to get married. Or why you have to do it so quickly.'

'Don't you think a woman would rather know ahead of time what she's getting into? I'd be annoyed as hell to discover my spouse had only married me to inherit money.'

'You have to tell them, of course, but not at the beginning, not before they have a chance to get to know you, to start feeling what a wonderful thing it would be to spend the rest of their lives as your wife.'

'That's not going to happen.' Which was why he now knew he couldn't marry Sam. She wanted more than he could offer. He couldn't give himself. If money wasn't enough, this endeavour was a waste of time.

'I believe it will.'

'I don't want to mislead anyone,' he said. 'This is tough enough without that.'

'You might find that you change your mind when you meet the right woman. It's been known to happen.'

'Women always think they can change a man.'

'Woman generally know what they're about.'

'You're a romantic,' he accused.

'Actually, I'm not.' Pain flickered

across her face. 'But I do believe it's possible to fall in love, even for someone who says he doesn't believe in it.'

'I didn't say I didn't believe in it. I said I didn't want it.' Not again. Not ever.

'You might not have a choice.'

'People always have a choice.'

Her face turned white.

With a sickening lurch, he recalled what Ruby had told him about Sam's husband. It was enough to allow him to guess what Sam must be feeling. Incredible to think she'd endured all she had, yet she still believed in romance.

'What would you have me do?' he asked more quietly.

'You know what to do.'

He reached for her hand, then stared down at it, stunned.

She gestured toward their linked fingers. 'You're already doing it.'

Swiftly, he released her. 'One has nothing to do with the other.'

'Being charming comes as naturally to you as song to a bird.'

'No one has ever accused me of being charming before.'

'It's not the sort of thing one says. It's the sort of thing one feels.'

'I did not hold your hand on purpose.'

'No, you did it by instinct.' She shook her head. 'I don't know why you even wanted me along.'

'I'm beginning to wonder that myself.'

'I can get off at the next port,' she offered.

'No, you can't.'

'What's to stop me?'

'Your grandmother. Your son.'

She stiffened.

He took her arm. 'Look, Sam, I'm sorry.'

'You're doing it again.'

'Doing what?'

'Touching me.' Her breath suddenly seemed uneven.

'I'm not doing it on purpose!'

'Which is exactly my point. Just do what you do naturally and you'll be fine.'

'Touching strange women is not something I do naturally.'

'You touch me.'

'I know you.'

'You don't know me,' she protested.

'I know you're honest and hard-working, funny and giving, that you love your family, that you're — '

Beautiful. He hadn't noticed until now just how beautiful.

Her hair was part of her beauty. It caught the sun like light on precious metal, and depending on the flitting shadows thrown by passers-by, alternated between gold and silver. But it was her eyes that mesmerized, their deep indigo seeming a barometer of her emotion. He hadn't realized in the office how much he watched her when she was with him, how much he depended on her . . .

He shook his head, tried to dislodge the thoughts and images swirling through his brain.

'I'm what?' she demanded.

'Nothing,' he muttered.

'Always right,' she suggested, with a grin.

'Always certain, seldom right,' he countered, breathing easier himself as the tension between them dissipated.

Her eyes grew serious. 'I'm right about this.'

'Then I'll have to trust you.' To his amazement, he found he did. 'You tell me what to do, and I'll do it.'

★   ★   ★

Sam flopped onto her bed and lay there with her eyes shut, oblivious to the clothes scattered around and beneath her. Thank goodness, Grams had offered to take Jamie up on deck. Her head was pounding so hard it seemed about to explode.

Which was what came of encouraging Nate to do what she could never do herself, to fake an emotion he didn't feel in order to get what he wanted. Despicable! Reprehensible! And it was all her own idea. With a groan, Sam covered her face with a pillow.

Someone tapped on the door.

She kept the pillow where it was and prayed whoever it was would go away. Probably the steward with those extra towels she had requested. In which case he'd just come in when he didn't hear her answer.

Another knock.

'Just a minute.' Her words were muffled by the pillow, but still boomed in her own ears.

'You O.K.? You sound — '

With another groan, she removed the pillow, her face now hot and sweaty from the warmth of the down feathers. Nate leaned against her cupboard, looking decidedly unruffled.

'How did you get in?' she demanded.

'You left your door unlocked.'

'An unlocked door is not an open invitation to enter.'

'A cry for help?' he asked.

'What do you mean?'

'Your feeble attempt to do away with yourself.' He cast a meaningful glance at the pillow clutched in her right hand.

'I just wanted some peace and quiet.'

'Hold that pillow where it was for long and you'll get more than peace and quiet.'

'What are you doing here?'

'Ruby asked me to look in on you. I met her and Jamie up by the pool.'

Maybe if she shut her eyes, he would simply disappear.

The bed dipped as he sat down beside her.

Her heart began to pound as hard as her head. He was too close, too intimate, sitting where he was, as though he were a friend . . . more than a friend.

'Ruby said you had a headache,' he commented solicitously.

She heard the sound of liquid splashing into a glass.

'I've brought you some aspirin.'

'I don't need any aspirin.' She kept

her eyes resolutely shut. 'I just want to sleep.'

'Take two of these first.'

'Go away!' she said desperately. She didn't want to feel what she was feeling, didn't know how to make it stop.

'You have to take care of yourself.'

'So that I can help you?' With a sigh, she opened her eyes.

'Partly,' he admitted, taking hold of her left hand. He gently opened her clenched fist and dropped two tablets into her palm.

'I never should have come.' She glared at him. 'You never should have asked me.'

'Feeling guilty about suggesting I lie?'

'No!' Yes. But she'd had no other choice. If she didn't find someone for him fast, it would be difficult to hide her own feelings, feelings she couldn't afford to examine, let alone possess.

'All right then. We'll make a start.'

'I'm not feeling very well — '

'I don't mean now. Get some rest first.' He handed her the water. 'Now swallow the pills and shut your eyes.'

With a thankful sigh, she did as he directed.

'Now lie back and go to sleep.'

'I can't sleep until you leave.' Even then it would be difficult.

'I'm not going anywhere — '

Her eyes snapped open.

' — until you're asleep.'

'I'm not a child.'

'I didn't say you were.'

'I can't get to sleep with you here.'

'I won't make a sound.'

'Besides — ' Heat crawled up her face. ' — Grams and Jamie might come back. What will they think if they find you here?'

'They'll be glad you're not alone if you're not feeling well. Besides,' he said firmly, 'they're exploring the ship. They won't be back for ages.'

'Nevertheless.'

His gaze left her face and drifted around her room, lighting on the clothing strewn over every conceivable surface. 'I don't know how you can sleep in all this mess,' he said.

'Years of practise.' Her gaze followed his. Half-empty suitcases occupied both chairs, and her makeup bag tilted half in and half out of the top drawer of her dresser.

Nate shook his head. 'I can't believe you managed to jam all this stuff into your bags!'

'I wasn't sure what I'd need.'

'So you brought everything?'

'Not completely.' She smiled. 'I didn't bring my winter jacket.'

'The one thing you could have used on the way to the airport.'

'Your jacket was warm enough,' she replied, with a chuckle.

'I'm glad you liked it.' His lips twitched also. 'But if you're going to take up travelling, you've got to get selective.'

'Why?'

'So you can carry the damn cases without getting a hernia.'

'I haven't had to carry them yet. All the airports have push carts, and once I checked my bags, I didn't see them again until we landed. At which point the cruise staff took care of them.' Her smile widened. 'I could've had twenty bags.'

'Where are you going to put everything?'

'There's plenty of closet space and drawers.'

'You haven't even started unpacking that duffle bag.'

'I can't go on a holiday without books.'

'Books,' he groaned. 'No wonder it was so heavy!'

'You only carried it from the house to the car.'

'That was far enough! On the way home, you can carry it yourself.'

'This trip has barely begun and you're already talking about going home!'

'I'm beginning to wish we'd never left.'

'Ditto!' She frowned. 'How did you get tickets at such short notice anyway?

I thought these Christmas cruises got booked months in advance.'

'Pulled in a favour.'

'Must have been a big one.'

'Someone who knew my great-uncle,' he said gruffly. 'Now are you going to go to sleep or shall I help you straighten up this mess?'

'Don't touch a thing.' But her order came too late. He had picked up the pile closest to him, and her black slip and bra slithered off the top and on to the floor. 'Give those to me,' she cried, holding out her arms.

He did as she asked, then before she could tell him no, he scooped up the fallen articles and handed those to her as well. Cheeks hot, she rose from her bed and flung them into the top drawer of her dresser.

'Let's get a cold drink,' she suggested, slipping her feet into her sandals.

'What about your nap?'

'Later,' she muttered, heading for the door. She needed out of the intimacy permeating this room, and more space around this man who made her feel things she shouldn't.

\*     \*     \*

She was looking better already, Nate reassured himself, glancing across the table at Sam. Her brow had lost its furrowed look and her shoulders were no longer glued against the back of her chair, forcing her spine ramrod-straight and her jawline tense. Even her eyes had regained their customary sparkle, and after one sweep of the Promenade deck's Parisian-styled bar, she had trained them on him.

'Seems a strange sort of Christmas Eve,' she said. 'No snow, no ice — '

'Sunshine instead, and warm weather — '

' — no last-minute shopping.'

'Any more shopping and they wouldn't have let us on the plane!'

'It's not all clothes in those bags. Most of the space is taken up by presents.'

'Why didn't you exchange gifts

before you left home?'

'Before Christmas?' she asked, her voice an outraged squeak.

'Easier than lugging everything three thousand miles.'

'But exchanging gifts ahead of time, it . . . it just wouldn't be Christmas.'

She said the word the way Jenny had always said it, as though it embodied all that was magical and good in the world.

'I suppose not,' Nate said, not wanting to think of Jenny, or Christmas, either. Since Jenny's death, the holiday had held no appeal. 'Jamie and Ruby looked as though they were having fun,' he said, determined to change the subject.

'They did, didn't they?' Sam agreed, smiling.

A beautiful, brilliant smile, radiating such warmth, Nate wished it was for him.

'Although Grams seemed to be giving that children's activities director a run for her money.'

Nate chuckled. 'You didn't tell me

Ruby had a killer table tennis serve.'

'Who knew?' Sam replied, her smile broadening to a grin.

'And the way she was eying that shuffleboard game — '

'I know. I'm almost afraid to go back and see how it's going.' Sam winced. 'When she slammed that ball back to that spiky-haired boy — '

'He didn't look as though he was enjoying being beaten by an old lady,' Nate replied, grinning back at Sam.

'Better not let Grams hear you call her that.'

'I wouldn't dare.'

'What about you?' Sam asked, her tone becoming suddenly serious.

'I could probably beat your Grandmother if I tried hard enough.'

'That's not what I meant.'

'No?'

'Do you see anyone in here that appeals to you?'

'I'm not on a hunt!'

'That's exactly what you're on!'

'Then the answer is no.' He gave the

room another glance. 'I don't see anyone here that I'd like to marry.'

Sam frowned. 'Don't think of it like that.'

'How am I supposed to think of it?'

'Just don't think about the marriage part, or you'll get tied up in knots.'

'I'm not nervous.'

'I know, but you don't really want to do this. If you start out thinking marriage, you'll put the kibosh on any desire to get to know these women.'

'So what do you suggest?'

'Look for someone who appeals — '

'I don't want anyone who appeals.'

' — talk to her. Buy her a drink. Flirt a little.'

'And then?'

'Just enjoy her company. Make sure she enjoys yours.'

'There's not enough time left to enjoy anything.' Although one part of him wished the time was completely gone, and that this damn fool quest was at an end.

'You can't just pop the question.

You've got to lead up to it, make the woman feel you care — '

'There's got to be some other way.'

' — although you run the risk of really beginning to care.'

'That will never happen.'

'It's the only way your crazy scheme is going to work!'

'Matchmakers in the movies never seem to worry about who likes whom,' he teased.

'Then hire yourself one.'

'I did.'

Her eyes flashed, sparks shooting through the air between them.

Nate pretended to pick up a fallen napkin, hiding his smile as he did so. When he re-emerged from beneath the table, she was waiting, arms folded.

'Well?' she demanded.

He gave a long-suffering sigh. 'How about the brunette in the corner?' he suggested.

She nodded. 'Go now. Get it over with.'

Thank God it wasn't her who had to

do what Nate was doing, going up to a stranger and sitting down and talking. She'd dished out the advice, but would have found it impossible to follow herself.

It wasn't that she was shy or overly critical of her own appearance — although she still hadn't shed the ten extra pounds she'd been carrying since her pregnancy with Jamie — but to initiate contact with a member of the opposite sex with matrimony in mind — Sam shuddered at the thought.

The brunette was smiling up at Nate with an appreciative gleam forming in her eyes. Sam frowned as Nate, looking pleased, waggled a finger to catch the waiter's eye. In the next instant the two were sitting at the woman's table, each holding a full glass of white wine.

Nate's companion was pretty, Sam decided glumly. Beautiful even, if you liked that long-legged, lean look. And from the attentive way Nate was listening to every word she said, she was obviously exactly his type.

Which meant Sam's job was done. She no longer had to sit there and watch her boss pursue his quarry. Only, somehow, her legs wouldn't do what she asked, and she couldn't shift, either, her gaze from Nate's back.

'Is this seat taken?'

Sam twisted around to find a man standing over her, muscles bulging beneath his tee shirt and swim trunks. *Kiss Me, I'm Cute* was emblazoned in purple and yellow on the front of his shirt.

'My name's Rex,' the man said, swinging his leg over the chair opposite. 'Rex Carson.' He winked. 'I noticed you earlier up on the Lido deck with that redhead.'

'Oh,' Sam replied weakly.

'Thought to myself, now there's a girl I'd like to get to know.'

'Me?' Sam asked. A giggle rose in her throat. 'Or the redhead?'

'You, of course. I don't go in much for redheads. My first wife had red hair — ' He shook his head. 'She was a firecracker. I couldn't take the heat.' He gazed appreciatively at Sam. 'Blondes are a different matter.'

'Always a mistake, I think, characterizing people by the colour of their hair.'

'Sexy,' he went on, as though she hadn't spoken. 'Likes a good time — '

'That 'blondes have more fun' adage is an old wives' tale,' Sam said firmly. 'Besides, I dye my hair this colour.'

Rex leaned closer and peered at her hair. 'Don't see no roots.'

'Just did it,' she lied.

'Don't see no ring on that finger, either.'

'She's with me, pal,' came a growl. Nate was suddenly there, his hand clamped on Rex's shoulder.

'Don't see you sitting here,' Rex muttered.

'I'm here now.'

'Looks like you've got all you can handle with that girlie over there.' Rex pointed at the brunette, then slowly rose, thrust out his chest, and seemed to dare Nate to contradict him.

'She's a friend of my fiancée,' Nate replied, indicating Sam with a nod. He didn't shift his gaze from Rex.

'Fiancée!' Sam exclaimed.

'Sounds like the little woman here don't know nothing about being engaged to you, Mister.'

'Not yet, maybe.' His eyes grew hard. 'This is our engagement cruise — ' He took a step closer. ' — and you've just spoiled it.'

Furious, Sam pushed back her chair and stood. 'Get lost,' she snapped at Nate. 'I don't need your help.' Glancing past him, she saw the brunette pick up her purse and head for the door.

'You heard the lady,' Rex said with a smirk.

'And I don't want a drink with you either,' Sam barked.

'But . . . ' the man spluttered.

Sam flung a tenner on the table, then turned on her heel and headed for the door.

'Catch you later, pretty lady,' Rex called after her.

All Sam heard next was the crunch of knuckles meeting a jaw.

# 6

'Are you nuts?' Sam demanded. She pushed Nate onto his bed and none-too-gently dabbed a wet cloth against the cut on his lip.

'Oomph,' he groaned. 'You were in trouble,' he added, when she pulled the cloth away.

'If that's what you call trouble, you've never been a woman.'

'No,' he admitted slowly.

'I was handling Rex just fine.'

'He was harassing you.'

'He was a stupid man who'd had too much to drink. I could have got rid of him with a snap of my fingers.'

'Then why didn't you?'

'Took a minute to figure out he was a jerk.'

'I could tell *that* just by looking at him.'

'Then I guess you're like most men.'

'What do you mean?'

'Making decisions based on outward appearances.' She touched his lip again, noting, with an involuntary flash of sympathy, that it was beginning to swell. 'You need some ice on that lip.'

'Forget the ice.'

She could scarcely hear his voice through the fold of the cloth. Then he reached up and took hold of her wrist, forcing her hand away from his lip.

Could he feel her racing pulse beneath his fingers? Sam shook off his hand, stepped around his suitcase and moved to the tiny refrigerator built into the wall beneath the safe. With a swift whack of the tray against the dresser top, she extracted some ice and wrapped it in the cloth.

'It's a cruise ship,' she continued, when she was once again seated beside him. 'People are friendly on cruise ships. That's the whole point.' She became uncomfortably aware of the proximity of his leg to hers.

'Not people on their honeymoon.'

'We're not on our honeymoon.'

'As far as that fool knew we could have been. Once I told him the way things stood, he should have — '

'What? Fled? For all you knew, he was simply a friendly guy looking to make some friends.'

'He made it clear what sort of friend he was after!' He shook his head. 'I can't believe you're defending him.'

'What about you? You were making something pretty clear yourself to that brunette.'

'Just doing what you told me to do.' He glanced at her shrewdly. 'What's the matter? Were you jealous?'

Sam gritted her teeth.

'Besides,' Nate continued, 'we were talking about her dog.'

'Right,' Sam replied, 'like her dog's going to be the first thing she discusses when a handsome man chats her up.'

'Handsome?'

'Some people might think so.'

'Do you?'

'It doesn't matter what I think! It's

not me you have to impress.'

'True.' He gazed at her thoughtfully.

'What matters right now is that we get one thing straight.'

'And that would be?'

'I'm not your sister, or your cousin, or — ' She held the words for a moment, not sure she could spit them out. ' — your fiancée. I don't want your protection, or your help.'

'Even when you need it?'

'You're the one who needs help.' She slapped the iced washcloth against his lip.

'I should have ducked,' he agreed, wincing beneath her onslaught. 'I never was very good against a right hook.'

'You didn't do so hot against his left hook, either.' Despite her best intentions, Sam couldn't stop a smile forming on her lips.

'At least he didn't get away scot free.'

'I don't think you can count him slipping on a wet spot the great fight-of-the-century move.'

'So next time you're in trouble?'

'Walk right on by.'

'You might regret it.'

'I doubt it.' She peered at his lip. 'Do you need a plaster on that?'

'You don't put plasters on lips.' He stood and peered into the mirror above his dresser. 'Makes it tricky when you kiss.'

'I thought you weren't intending to kiss anyone.' Sam's throat turned dry at the thought of him kissing someone else. She had to get control, couldn't allow herself to care who he made love to or married.

'Just because I don't want to be in love with the woman I marry, doesn't mean I don't want to kiss her.'

'What about the brunette?' Sam tried to smooth the creases she could feel forming above her nose. 'Or have you completely ruined your chances with her by leaping to my defence?'

'She owns a poodle,' he explained solemnly. 'I could never marry anyone who owns a poodle.'

'What's wrong with poodles?'

'Their owners talk about them incessantly.'

Sam stifled a grin. 'So you didn't click?'

'I'm still looking.'

He was looking at her, and in a way that made her suddenly realize she was still sitting on his bed. Abruptly, she rose.

'So what's next?' he asked quietly.

'Next?' She wrested her gaze from the magic of his eyes and let it scan his room. 'You haven't unpacked yet, either. Better do that.'

'Care to help?'

'You can manage.' But she picked up a pile of silky somethings and prepared to fling them into an open drawer.

'It'll be time for dinner soon.' He took a step closer.

'Christmas Eve,' she said hoarsely.

'Christmas Eve,' he repeated. Pain flickered across his eyes, was audible in his voice.

She held out her hand, finding it impossible to stop this gesture of comfort. Was he thinking of his wife? Or of his child? Or of never again being able to spend Christmas with either?

All at once, she touched him, her fingers finding his in a connection so electric her skin seemed to burn. In that same instant came fear. Fear of wanting him, of needing him, in a way she hadn't allowed herself to need anyone since Phil.

His hand tightened on hers, and the pupils of his eyes seemed to expand and grow darker. His expression grew darker, too, as though his brain dictated distance as much as hers did.

But the pull of body to body was too strong to deny and with a smooth movement, they were in each other's arms.

Sam opened her mouth, but the only sound to emerge was a stifled moan. She pulled her gaze from Nate's but it lighted on his lips instead, which were moulded fully and firmly into a shape that drew her in. The anticipation of his kiss was as exciting as it was excruciating, and from the naked yearning in his eyes, she knew he felt it too.

He held her loosely, as though he, too, fought desire. Every inch of her that faced him longed to feel him closer, while at the same time recognized how dangerous was that need.

Slowly, ever slowly, his lips drew nearer, until at last they touched with the merest brushing of skin to skin. Their breaths mingled and in that moment so did their souls, sending through Sam's body the sensation of coming home.

Except there was no coming home with this man, for he intended to marry for one reason only, to spend a lifetime with a woman in order to inherit the money he needed to keep his business secure.

Sam's future, too, depended on that inheritance, was hanging in the chasm between solvency and ruin. She had to keep her mind on that, cling to what she knew, then perhaps the need she felt for Nate would disappear.

But despite her determination, she kissed him back, and her kisses were as eager as his.

'Mom!' a voice cried, then repeated the word again, until finally it filtered clearly through the blanket of heat surrounding them.

As intrusive as the cry, came a rapping on the door.

'Are you in there, mom?'

Two breaths pulled in as one, and in that same oneness, Nate separated from Sam, leaving her soul as naked as a bird without feathers.

'I'm here, Jamie,' she called, staring into Nate's eyes. She was unable to read them now, couldn't tell if he welcomed or cursed the interruption. She dared not examine her own feelings on the subject, for fear of discovering what she'd find.

'Whatcha doing?' Jamie called.

'Nothing,' Sam said breathlessly. She could hear Grams now also, softly murmuring to Jamie.

'Come in,' Sam said, still holding Nate's silky somethings. 'I'm just helping Nate unpack.'

Jamie opened the unlocked door and galloped into Nate's room, his face and feet alive with the excitement of his day. Ruby followed more slowly, and her expression grew thoughtful as she glanced from Nate to Sam.

'What're you doing with Nate's underwear?' Jamie asked, with a giggle.

Sam stared at the objects in her hand then flung the offending boxers back at their owner. 'I think I'll finish my own unpacking now.' She felt her face flame. 'We'll see you later, Nate. Say in the dining room about eight o'clock?' Without waiting for his answer, she took hold of Jamie's hand, threw her grandmother a pleading look and tried not to run as she exited the cabin.

★   ★   ★

'You and Nate seemed to be having a good time,' Sam's grandmother ventured when they were safely back in Sam's room.

'I wouldn't call it a good time exactly.' Sam averted her face from her grandmother's all-knowing eyes, and turned to the suitcase on her bed. She plucked out a fistful of tee shirts and stuffed them into the second drawer of her dresser.

'Did Jamie and I interrupt something?' Ruby asked bluntly.

Sam cast Jamie a hasty glance, but she needn't have worried. Her son was sitting by the window with his back towards them, engrossed by the beeps emanating from his hand-held video game, and shouting as the cartoon heros fought to save the princess.

'No,' Sam denied.

'Didn't look like nothing,' Grams ventured.

'That's all it was.'

'It looked as though you'd been kissing.'

Sam's cheeks flushed. She should

have known it was futile lying to her grandmother. Her own mother had told her as much when she was still alive. But Sam had hoped that the drastically changing times of the modern world would baffle the old woman, would render her incapable of believing her granddaughter would be kissing a man she wasn't involved with, especially in the man's bedroom.

'He looks as though he knows a thing or two about kissing,' her grandmother went on with an appreciative smile.

'Grams!' Sam protested.

'Your grandfather was an excellent kisser.' Ruby's eyes turned dreamy. 'He made my insides turn to mush.'

'He did?' Sam stared at her grandmother's face, probing past the wrinkles to the ageless woman inside.

'Is that how it felt when Nate kissed you?' Her grandmother's faraway look had disappeared, leaving her eyes bright as she held Sam's gaze.

'Yes,' Sam whispered, stunned at how easily the truth had spilled forth.

'Which is why it can never happen again.'

'Why not? Nate's a fine figure of a man.'

'Yes, he is, but — '

'He's not only handsome, good-natured, and the Lord knows, generous, he's — '

'He doesn't believe in love,' Sam said flatly. 'So that's that.'

'What makes you think he doesn't?'

'He told me so.'

Her grandmother laughed. 'You'd be a fool to believe everything a man tells you.'

'Am I supposed to ignore trust and honesty?'

'Men don't always say what they really think — '

'He thinks it all right.'

' — because they don't know what they really think,' her grandmother finished. 'A woman's only hope is to go by her instincts.' Ruby's eyes probed hers. 'How did it feel when you kissed?'

Like she'd been transported to

another world, where all thought was suspended and only feelings counted.

'Pleasant,' Sam replied, pushing away that other knowledge. 'But kissing isn't enough.'

'It's a first step,' Grams said dryly.

'I want more than that — '

'Like what?'

'Love, commitment — '

'That comes later.'

'Not ever, according to Nate.'

'He's just frightened. Most men are by what they don't understand.'

'Nate knows what he wants.'

'And what's that?'

Sam opened her mouth to speak, then immediately closed it again. She couldn't discuss the true purpose of Nate's voyage, or confess her own part in it either.

'He's not getting any younger,' her grandmother mused.

'He's not even thirty yet!'

'Perhaps he wants to get married.'

'He was married.'

'Was he?' Her grandmother frowned.

'Where's his wife now?'

'She died,' Sam said softly.

'Then that's all the more reason for him to get married again. It's not healthy to be alone in life.' Ruby stared at Sam sternly. 'You'd do well to remember that.'

'I'm not alone.'

'You know what I'm talking about.'

'A man, you mean?'

'Of course a man.'

'I'm not getting married just so I won't be alone. When I marry again, it'll be to a man who wants to commit, who wants to spend a lifetime with me and Jamie. Not one who'll leave when the going gets tough.'

'Nate could be that kind of man.'

'You don't know him.'

Her grandmother settled into her chair with the air of one ready to listen. 'So tell me about him.'

'I told you what I know, what he feels about love.'

'It seems the two of you must have been close if you've already discussed it. Men don't talk lightly about things like that.'

'Nate has his reasons.'

'Which are?'

'You'll have to ask him.' Then, horrified at her suggestion, she cried, 'No, don't!'

'But what *does* he want?' Ruby asked. 'Have you discussed that?'

'I . . . I . . . '

Her grandmother's eyebrows narrowed to a point above her nose. 'There's something you're not telling me, child. What is it?'

Sam swallowed hard. Another glance at Jamie assured her the child was still engrossed in his game, would offer no lifeline now when she needed him.

'Spit it out dear,' Ruby commanded. 'A trouble shared is a trouble halved.'

'Not this time, Grams.' Sam hid a smile at the homily her grandmother had spouted. Something Ruby always did when she wanted her own way. 'It's not my trouble. It's not mine to discuss.'

'But it has to do with Nate?'

'Yes,' she admitted.

'Then it's your business too,' Ruby said firmly. 'Now don't look at me as though I'm an old fool who doesn't know what she's talking about! I've seen the way you look at that young man.'

'What do you mean?' Panic fluttered in Sam's chest. Her grandmother had the intuition of a witch when it came to matters of the heart, but she'd thought that now she was older she was better at hiding how she felt. She couldn't bear to think she was an open book for Ruby to read.

'You like him,' her grandmother said simply. 'No matter how much you try to tell yourself differently.'

'Of course I like him. I work for him.'

'I mean *like* him!'

'It doesn't matter whether I like him or not, Grams.'

'Of course it matters.'

'He wants to get married again — '

'That's wonderful.'

'For money,' Sam added harshly. 'Not for love.' She regretted the words the moment they escaped her lips, couldn't bear the disappointment in her grandmother's eyes, or the sudden fragility in her bearing.

'What do you mean?' the old woman asked.

'He needs a wife, Grams,' Sam explained. 'Just as you said he did, but not because he wants a partner with whom to share his life, but because he'll inherit twenty million dollars if he marries.'

'I don't understand.'

'His great-uncle Edward left him twenty million dollars in his will, on the condition Nate marries by his thirtieth birthday.'

'Which is when?'

'January the first.'

'Which leaves him — ' Her grand-mother counted on her fingers. 'Eight days! And that's counting today which is already half over.'

'Not nearly enough time.'

'You can fall in love in an instant,'

Ruby said firmly.

'Maybe, but he's not marrying for love.'

'So what's your part in all of this?'

'I said I'd help. Which is why we're all here. He insists that he's forgotten how to flirt and asked that I teach him.' She smiled ruefully. 'He had no difficulty earlier up on deck.'

'Flirting's like riding a bicycle,' her grandmother said complacently. 'Once you learn, you never forget.'

'I don't know about that.' Sam sighed. 'I'm beginning to think I'm just as rusty.'

'It has been ages since you've been out on a date.'

'I haven't met anyone I want to date.'

'You have now,' Grams said softly.

'You can't mean — '

'Nate.'

'No,' Sam said firmly. 'I can't risk it. Not for myself — ' She glanced at her son and her resolve strengthened. ' — or for Jamie.'

'Not every marriage is destined to

turn out like your first one.'

'I'm going to make damn sure it doesn't!'

'Just don't shut down on something wonderful before you know what you're throwing away.'

'I know what I'm doing, Grams.'

'Well I'm going to think about it, too.' The old woman pursed her lips thoughtfully.

'Grams!' Sam exclaimed. 'I absolutely forbid you to interfere.'

'Would I do that?'

'I don't trust you.'

'It seems like you don't trust anyone.' Her grandmother leaned forward and touched Sam on the knee. 'I only want what's best for you, Samantha. You know that.'

'But who's deciding what's best for me, Grams? Me?' Her eyebrow cocked. 'Or you?'

'With great age comes great wisdom,' her grandmother pronounced cheerfully.

Sam groaned.

# 7

She was late. Sam peered through the glass doors leading into the main dining hall. They'd all be in there by now; Nate, Grams, and Jamie. Plus whoever else the head waiter had placed at their table.

Sam had asked her grandmother to take Jamie and go on without her. She had needed time to herself, time to think.

But the thinking hadn't produced any of the answers she sought, had raised nothing in her mind but more questions, the uppermost of which was how to keep her grandmother from interfering in whatever this thing was she had with Nate.

Like keeping a bone from a dog, Sam decided glumly. If her grandmother buried her teeth into Nate's business, he wouldn't stand a chance. The only answer was to get him married off, and fast!

But before she could do that, she had to talk to him, had to express as plainly as she could why the kisses they had shared had to stop, why, against all her body demanded, their relationship couldn't turn physical.

Sam pasted a smile on her lips and swept into the dining room, catching a distorted glimpse of her reflection in the glass doors as she passed through. She ran her hand through her curls in an effort to subdue the wildness the sea air had wrought, but her efforts only rendered her hair all the more unruly.

She spotted Nate first in a sea of heads floating in a backdrop of damask tablecloths. He was sitting with her family, leaning towards Jamie as though listening hard to what he said. Her grandmother watched them, smiling that secret smile that always bode trouble.

Table 61. Smack dab in the middle of the room. A big circular table around which there were ten chairs, only one of which still stood empty.

Nate suddenly looked up, and his gaze met hers. He rose and pulled out the chair beside him, waiting as she wended her way through the crowd.

'We were wondering where you'd got to,' he said when she arrived.

'Just taking my time.'

He cast her an appreciative glance. 'Worth it,' he complimented her softly.

'My mom's always late,' Jamie announced between bites of a cracker, from which the caviar had been carefully scraped and pushed to a corner of his plate.

'Not always,' Sam denied.

'Women like to make themselves beautiful,' Nate explained to Jamie with a wink.

'Not my mom,' the boy protested.

Once glance at Nate's face told Sam he didn't agree with her son. Heat prickled the base of her spine.

Nate cleared his throat and gestured toward the passengers clustered around the table. 'We were just getting introduced.'

Sam smiled at the strangers, grateful to divert the attention focussed on her. But Nate's hand still held her chair, and as she sat down, his fingers touched briefly and warmly against her back. Startled by the heat, she leaned forward at once and turned to the silver-haired gentleman sitting next to her grandmother.

'Charles Davidson,' the gentleman said, extending a well-manicured hand. 'I'm delighted to make your acquaintance.'

Sam smiled and connected her fingers to his.

'And this is Madeline and Elwood Payson — ' Nate indicated a middle-aged couple. ' — and Lindsay and David Green — ' The second pair held hands like newlyweds, barely sparing Sam a glance before retreating back into their private world. ' — and Fay Miller, of course, you know.'

Startled, Sam peered past Nate to the

woman sitting on his other side. How could she have missed Fay with her fiery hair swept up into a sleek chignon and her black dress showing off her svelte figure to perfection?

'Isn't this wonderful luck, darling?' Fay exclaimed. She stretched past Nate to pat Sam's arm. 'I had a word in the head waiter's ear, and he changed my seating to your table.'

'Wonderful,' Sam echoed, mustering what she hoped would pass for an enthusiastic smile. She had to talk to Nate, had hoped to do so at dinner. She'd never have a chance now in front of all these people.

'Did you see the Santa Claus made out of ice when you came in, Mom?' Jamie asked excitedly, placing his half-eaten cracker back on his plate. Only the edges had been nibbled. The middle portion, where the caviar had actually rested, lay discarded along with the fish roe.

'I did,' Sam replied, turning to her son with relief. At least *he* was loving

142

the trip. For Jamie's sake, she had to get her emotions under control, had to do for Nate what she'd been brought along to do, and at the same time make this Christmas the best she and her family had ever had.

'There'll be Christmas carols later,' she whispered in Jamie's ear. 'Out on deck — '

'So the fish can hear?' he asked excitedly.

'Something like that.' She smiled and touched his hand. 'But after that, you've got to go to bed. You don't want Santa catching you up.'

'Nate says Santa will be coming here later than Seattle.'

'Why's that?' she asked, glancing in Nate's direction. He didn't even notice, was too busy chatting to Fay in a companionable murmur. When had her boss spoken to Jamie about Santa Claus? And who'd asked him anyway to explain the ins and outs of the Christmas elf to her child?

'Nate says Santa likes people to have

fun at Christmas,' Jamie went on, 'and because he knows people are enjoying themselves on a cruise, he saves us for last.' He looked trustingly up at her. 'So we don't have to go to bed and miss anything,' he finished hopefully.

Before she could respond, Jamie took a sip from his Coke and turned to his great-grandmother with a satisfied sigh.

Sam poked Nate in the arm. 'Jamie says you said he could stay up late,' she accused, when he turned to face her. 'I didn't hear you asking me.'

'You can join us if you want,' Nate offered smoothly.

'You know what I mean!'

'Staying up a little later won't do the kid any harm.'

'Even I go to bed early on Christmas Eve.'

'And you call yourself a Christmas fanatic!' he scoffed.

'I'm not a fanatic of any kind!'

'If you go to bed, you'll miss the best part of Christmas.'

'The morning's the best part.'

'Not nearly as exciting as the night before,' he countered. 'All the anticipation, the mystery — '

'Jamie's only eight. He'll get overtired.'

'Don't worry about that. I'll help take care of him tomorrow.'

'That's not what I was suggesting.' Then suddenly aware of how harsh her voice must sound, she added in a softer tone, 'You won't have time.'

'There's all the time in the world.'

'Not if you intend to find a wife.'

'I've heard,' he replied, a dimple flashing on his cheek, 'that women find a man with a child attractive.'

'You are not using my son as a babe magnet! Besides, it's not men with kids women find enticing, it's men with babies.'

His smile disappeared as though she'd struck him, and the image of Nate's pregnant wife suddenly pierced Sam's brain, as did the knowledge of the baby in his dead wife's belly. A baby he'd never hold, never get to love.

'I'm sorry,' she whispered.

'It doesn't matter.'

But the expression in his eyes told her it did.

'It was a long time ago.'

It would never be long enough. 'I — '

'Forget it.' He leaned across her to speak to Jamie, and his shoulder touched her breast.

She knew he could feel nothing through the bulk of his dinner jacket, but electricity spiralled through her.

'They've got a kid's menu,' he told her son. 'How would you like a burger?'

'Will it have that black stuff on it?' Jamie asked, grimacing at the caviar still sitting on his plate.

'Nothing on it but what you order,' Nate promised. 'How about cheese and ketchup? That's how I like mine.'

'Great!' Jamie replied. 'What about fries?'

'Coming right up.' Raising his hand, Nate caught the waiter's attention. 'Cheeseburger and fries,' he ordered, when the man drew near, 'and chocolate cake for dessert.' He shot Jamie a swift grin. 'Better make that two.'

\* \* \*

The last time he'd seen this many stars was the weekend he and Jenny had taken that trip to Las Vegas and their car had broken down in the desert. Damned vehicle, he'd thought at the time, kicking its front tyre. Then he'd looked up at the sky and felt a lump in his throat, which grew even larger when he glanced into his wife's eyes and saw the stars reflected there like pinpricks of light on a black velvet canvas.

They'd made love under those stars, had been filled with joy. Staring at the heavens now, Nate again felt their magic, and was suddenly convinced that he could be happy a second time. In confusion, he looked at Sam and saw the stars in her eyes, too, saw the magic encase her in a golden light.

'It's beautiful,' she said, echoing the

words in his heart.

'Yes,' he replied hoarsely.

Then the ship's entertainment troupe slid into a chorus of *Silent Night*. While their voices caressed the air, the single violin accompanying them curled around the waves splashing the side of the boat then soared upward toward the heavens.

'Look!' Jamie whispered. He pointed skyward as a comet flashed across the sky, leaving a tail as bright as an arrow. 'It's Santa!' he cried, his voice filled with awe.

Nate squeezed the boy's shoulder in a silent communion of wonder. Then Sam's hand dropped onto his, and the spell between them intensified.

He dared not look at her, dared not see in her eyes what he feared was in his. But despite his best intentions, he couldn't make himself obey.

Her eyes were wide open, and her lips were parted. She appeared at this moment the most vulnerable creature on earth. Nate's grip tightened on

Jamie's shoulder.

'Ow,' the boy said. He squirmed from Nate's grasp and moved to the railing.

Sam faced Nate then and he saw again in her face the reflection of the universe, saw the trembling of her lips and the need in her eyes.

'We have to talk,' she said, her voice as shaky as the hand she suddenly withdrew.

'We've been talking all evening.'

'Not about this.'

'Then about what?'

'You know about what,' she whispered.

'If I know, why discuss it?'

'We have to be clear.'

'Fine,' he said.

'Not here,' she added, as though here was as impossible for her as it was for him.

'Where then?' He swiftly surveyed his surroundings. 'Behind the smokestack?'

'Of course not.' Colour tracked her cheeks.

'In one of the lifeboats, perhaps?' He

made light of her proposal, tried to convince himself his heart wasn't pounding faster at the thought of being alone with her.

'If you're not going to take this seriously — '

'Where, then?' he asked quietly, capitulating to the desperate look in her eyes.

'The Lizard Lounge,' she replied.

'When?'

'Midnight.' She glanced at her son. 'After I get Jamie to bed.'

\* \* \*

She'd been a fool to suggest that he meet with her here, in this light-dimmed room with a sequin-covered singer mewling soul tunes in the corner. She'd been a fool to ask to meet with him at all. Especially tonight when she was so exhausted, a condition that always led her to say things she shouldn't.

She'd been in just such a state the

night Phil left, had been up all the previous night and the whole day, too, rocking Jamie in her arms in an attempt to soothe his colic. When Phil began complaining about the tiny baby's crying, she'd been unable to stop herself from snapping that that was what babies did sometimes, especially when they were new, and that if Phil didn't like it he should leave, because he wasn't helping anything by standing around criticizing.

Phil had done as she suggested, had angrily stuffed his clothes into a suitcase, stating, while he packed, in a cold, furious voice, that no man should have to put up with a crying baby, a tired wife, and no dinner on the table when he came home.

But something in the way he said it made her feel he'd been looking for an excuse to do exactly what he wanted. And what he wanted was to leave. She had sensed that in him from the day they got married.

His final shot was that other women

appreciated a man's needs, and other women put their husbands first. Her heart had turned cold, for she knew he was referring to Susie Kellerman, the girl Phil had been dating before he met her. Susie had warned Sam on their wedding day that she'd do anything necessary to get Phil back.

But even knowing that her husband of less than a year was heading to the arms of another woman was not enough to induce Sam to beg him to stay, for she knew in her heart that Phil would leave Susie, too, for that's what Phil was like. No amount of wishing could change him into something better.

Which was why her grandmother was wrong when she suggested Nate could change. People didn't change. Not enough to take a chance.

Which was why she had to stifle the feelings she'd begun to have for Nate, had to set him straight about their kissing, and push him as swiftly as possible into the arms of the nearest marriageable woman.

With a sigh, Sam took a long sip of ice water. She hadn't ordered a drink for she needed a clear head to make this conversation go as she intended. She didn't want to risk an alcohol-induced setting aside of barriers and letting in of strangers.

Nate suddenly emerged from the shadows behind her. 'Sorry to keep you waiting.' He slipped into the chair opposite.

'No problem,' Sam replied.

'I was talking with someone. I didn't notice the time.' He stretched out his hand and shifted the candle from the middle of the table so it no longer blazed between them.

'Oh?' she answered. She had no intention of engaging in polite conversation. She wanted only to get on with it, to have her say, then disappear.

'Hm,' he replied. 'Pleasant woman.'

Jealousy, unexpected and sharp, flailed Sam like a whip. 'So you've met someone?'

'At the midnight buffet.'

'How could you possibly eat anything more after that huge dinner we had earlier?'

'Must be all the stargazing.'

She didn't want to remember standing beside him on deck, with the sky above sprinkling its magic in a glittering shower of moonlight and stardust.

'Hope you got the woman's name,' she said, forcing her attention back to the present.

'Rachel,' Nate answered, with an irritating promptness. 'Interesting woman.'

'I thought you didn't care what they were like.'

'They?'

'These women you're so intent on dating.'

'Who said anything about a date?'

'Surely you've set up a time to see her again?'

'I did suggest that perhaps sometime tomorrow — '

'Sometime! You've got to be more specific.' Sam took a deep breath. She had to handle this problem as she would those at work. 'Women don't like ambiguity,' she finally added.

'I thought spontaneity was the modern woman's criteria for good dating potential?'

'Further on in a relationship, perhaps, but in the beginning most women want a set time, a set place — '

'Boring.'

' — otherwise it doesn't feel like a date.'

'Not everything has to feel like a date.'

'If you intend to get married within eight days, you had better make sure that it does!'

'I don't think I'll be marrying Rachel.'

'Why not?'

'Her record's not so good — '

'She has a record?' Trust Nate to fall for a jailbird.

Trust any man. Looks were all men were interested in these days. That and the ability to still function at three in the morning, despite hair limp from dancing, and too many wine spritzers.

Maybe it was all in the attitude. Maybe attitude was what *she* needed.

No. She didn't want a man who wanted a woman like this Rachel person, a woman who wouldn't know how to commit if her life depended on it.

'Let's dance,' she suggested, not having the heart anymore to talk of Nate's mysterious conquest. Not wanting now, either, to investigate the whys and wherefores of Nate kissing her. Or of how she had kissed him back.

Dancing, she wouldn't have to look into his eyes and remember the desire she'd seen there before. Desire she couldn't return, for desire without commitment was like honey without bread; too sweet, too addictive, too downright dangerous.

Then Nate's arms drew her close and she knew dancing was a mistake.

Nate felt her body shiver as he touched the small of her back. But her skin was warm and welcoming and it was all he could do not to caress it with his hand.

'You wanted to talk?' he said, whispering the words.

She stiffened against his arm. He pulled away slightly and stared into her eyes. They were as luminous in their centres as two moons in the midnight sky.

'No,' she said uncertainly.

'Fine then.'

'It's not fine.'

'I just meant, so long as you're happy — '

'My happiness is not your responsibility.'

Any sane man would feel grateful she'd let him off the hook. Any sane man would run a mile from the feelings she invoked.

Too bad he wasn't sane.

'It's because of me you're on this cruise,' he said. 'I want you to have a good time.'

'Then shut up and dance.'

'The kiss,' he went on tersely. Perhaps if they did talk about the kiss, the fire in his loins would disappear. Then his gaze drifted to her lips, and the heat flared hotter.

Any plan to smother fire with reality seemed suddenly ridiculous, for he had ignored the one fact of which he'd been certain from the beginning. That Sam Feldon was not a woman for whom he could afford to care.

'The kiss,' she repeated, her eyes searching his.

His grip tightened, but he couldn't be sure whether he was pulling her closer or pushing her away.

'The kiss,' she said again, but more faintly this time, and her eyes seemed to hold the glaze of one hypnotized.

The music itself was enough to induce that state. It ensnared his mind and pulsated through his body, moving him, enticing him, making him long for things that seemed out of reach.

He brushed his lips across her neck. 'There you are!'

Nate's head jerked up.

'I was hoping to see you before tomorrow,' the voice continued.

'Rachel,' Nate said.

Feeling as though doused by a bucket of water, Sam pulled away from Nate. He still held her waist, but was staring past her now, over her shoulder.

Sam twisted around to look.

'Rachel Straus,' the woman said, introducing herself to Sam, but instead of holding out her hand for shaking, she tapped Sam's shoulder instead. 'You don't mind if I cut in? Nate promised me a dance.'

'Oh course not,' Sam said, backing away. 'Help yourself.'

'I'll just go along to the Ladies' room first.' Rachel winked. 'I shouldn't have had that last Tequila Sunrise.'

'*That's* Rachel!' Sam exclaimed, the minute the other woman had departed.

'Yes.'

'The woman you met at the buffet?'

'Only Rachel I know.'

'But I was expecting — '

'What?'

'She's old!'

'I wouldn't let her catch you saying that!'

'You said she had a record!'

'A track record,' Nate responded patiently. 'At eighty-five you have to expect that.'

'Eighty-five!'

'She looks more like ninety,' he added with a chuckle, 'but she's got the energy of a woman a quarter-century her junior.'

'I'm not sure I've got that kind of energy now!'

'I think you do,' Nate murmured, reaching for her again.

'What sort of track record?' Sam persisted, taking a step backward to keep out of reach.

'Marriage, of course.' He smiled at her ruefully. 'And you wonder why I don't believe in love.'

'If you don't tell me what you mean — ' She glared at him and moved closer. ' — I'm going to step on your toes!'

'I wouldn't do that,' he warned. 'Rachel's expecting a dance.'

Sam raised her right foot and poised it threateningly over his.

'She's been married five times,' he answered hastily.

'*Five* times!'

'And she's had three offers since her last husband died, but she says she doesn't want to go through all that again. She says she's had enough of looking after old men. What she wants now is a younger man to live with, one who's willing to do her laundry and take her dancing on Saturday nights.'

'Does she think you might be that younger man?'

'No,' he denied hastily. 'She's thinking more of a sixty- or seventy-year-old.'

Sam couldn't stop the giggles bubbling up her throat.

'She's only dancing with me because she thinks it'll be good for her image.'

'And why are you dancing with her?'

'Because I like her,' he said firmly.

'Sounds like Rachel should be the one giving you dating tips! Not me!'

'I'll stick with you.' Nate captured her this time before she could evade him.

The warmth in his eyes made Sam's heart beat faster.

'According to Rachel's theory,' he added in a low voice, 'being seen with a beautiful younger woman is the secret of success.'

'I'm not that much younger.'

'But you are beautiful.'

She drew back in surprise. Nate looked surprised, also, as though as stunned as she by what he'd just said.

'Perhaps we should talk about that kiss,' Sam reminded him.

A frown creased his forehead.

'I know it didn't mean anything,' Sam began.

'If it meant nothing, what is there to discuss?'

'I just don't think it's a good idea to

be kissing each other.'

'You were keen that I kiss Chrissy St. Claire.'

'That was different. You were dating her.'

'We went out once. It was hardly the romance of the century.'

'We're not going out at all.' Though the rush of blood pulsing through her veins made her feel as though they were.

'But you are my advisor on all things personal.'

'That doesn't mean I have to kiss you.'

'I had the impression you enjoyed it.'

'You're wrong! I didn't!' If she'd been Pinocchio, she'd be tripping over her nose.

'I could have sworn you kissed me back.' He leaned towards her as though to repeat the process.

'You caught me off guard.' Not something that was going to happen again.

'You said you'd be my coach.'

'You said nothing about kissing.'

'I told you I was rusty.'

'Not at kissing.'

'So you did enjoy it.' His smile now was smug.

'I didn't say that!'

'You told me yourself women like a little romance.'

'There's more to romance than kissing!'

'But kissing's the most fun.'

It had been more than fun, but she couldn't afford a repetition.

'Practise makes perfect,' he suggested softly.

'Practise on someone else!'

'Who exactly? The woman in the bar? Fay?'

Infuriatingly, when he put it like that, she couldn't stomach the idea of him kissing another woman.

'Whoever!' she snapped, forcing the image from her mind. 'Just so long as it's not me!'

# 8

Had she stayed up all night, she couldn't have been more exhausted. For that she blamed Nate.

If he hadn't danced with her, hadn't made her feel in his arms what she couldn't afford to feel with a man like him, hadn't kissed her . . . she wouldn't have been up all night twisting her bed sheets into a tangled mess.

She'd finally fallen asleep when the first light showed on the horizon, only to be wakened by Jamie bursting into her room.

'Merry Christmas!' he cried, flopping onto her bed. He gave her a sloppy kiss. 'Santa came!' he continued, his eyes lit up like the lights on the Christmas tree. 'Come see!'

'Is Grams up?' Sam pressed her fingers against the back of her neck in an effort to still the throbbing in her head. Another thing for which she could thank Nate.

'She's been up for ages,' Jamie answered, in a voice rising with excitement.

'Jamie,' she begged, pressing her eyes shut. Perhaps if she kept them closed, Christmas could be postponed for an hour. 'You'll wake the people next — '

'Are you coming?' he persisted, giving her hand another tug.

With a sigh, she capitulated. The pounding in her head now spread to her neck.

'Get my housecoat,' she ordered wearily, stifling the desire to crawl back under her covers and not emerge until the New Year.

Jamie snatched up her blue silk robe, and placed it awkwardly around her shoulders.

'Wait 'til you see, Mom,' he continued, when that was done. 'There are so many presents!'

Jamie's enthusiasm warmed Sam despite her fatigue. She'd been shopping for weeks, had wanted this

Christmas to be the best her son had ever had. A model car, a baseball, the puzzle he'd been admiring of animals in a jungle, had been just a few of the things she had purchased. Little gifts were all they were, but each one was special, for when she had bought them, her heart had been filled with love.

'Merry Christmas, Jamie,' she said softly, reaching out to hug him.

'Aw, Mom,' he replied, wiggling away from her caress. 'Let's go.'

'I thought we were going to open our gifts here.'

'We can't,' Jamie exclaimed. 'You've got to come see.' Again he tugged her fingers.

'All right, all right,' she said with a chuckle. She crawled out of bed and followed him into the hall. But when she got to the room Jamie shared with her grandmother, Sam stopped in her tracks.

Over by the window, positioned so the tropical sun bathed it in light, stood a decorated tree. Not a Christmas tree like the one they had at home, but a glorious olive tree, its roots buried in earth. Festooning its branches were strands of lights, all of them twinkling against the tree's blue-green leaves. And on the very top, amongst the new growth of the uppermost branch, a silver star precariously perched.

More astonishing than that was the man crouched at the tree's foot.

'Nate!' Sam exclaimed.

'Merry Christmas,' he said, smiling.

'Where did it come from?' Sam asked. She couldn't stop staring at the tree, was unable to take in the sensations shooting through her.

Nate wasn't family. He wasn't even a friend. Yet here he was in his dressing gown, standing in her son's bedroom, sharing their Christmas morning as though he belonged.

With a clench of her heart, Sam realized how easily he did belong, how he'd inserted himself into her life, into her family's life, too. How he'd changed the tradition set up since before Jamie was born and taken them on board this ship as though it were the most natural thing in the world. And despite the fact they weren't at home, had ensured the magic of Christmas morning.

'Santa brought it,' Jamie whispered, staring at the tree in awe. 'It wasn't here last night. I put my presents to you and Grams next to the window and when I woke, there they all were under the tree.'

'Wow!' Sam said, smiling gratefully at Nate.

His own smile growing, he held out a present.

'Mine first,' Jamie exclaimed, crouching down next to Nate and eagerly turning over various shapes and sizes of gifts.

'Don't just stand there,' Ruby admonished Sam from her chair next to her bed. 'Come in and shut the door.'

'This one's from me!' Jamie cried, bringing Sam a present wrapped as tightly as Fort Knox.

Sam sank onto her son's bed and turned the box over in her hands. From its size, shape, and weight it might be anything from a pair of shoes to a gaily wrapped rock.

'Open it,' Jamie commanded. Colour blazed his cheeks.

Sam slipped her fingers beneath the tape, until all the paper seemed to come loose at once, revealing the knobby surface of a purple clay pot.

'I made it,' her son said proudly, pointing out the daisy he'd painted on the pot's side. 'It's for flowers.' He glanced at her anxiously. 'You like flowers,' he added, as though to remind her.

'It's beautiful,' Sam exclaimed, running her hand over its uneven surface. 'Just look at the glazing.' She smiled at Jamie. 'Did you do that too?'

'All of it,' he said. 'My teacher said it was the best in the class.'

'I love it,' Sam said. A lump formed in her throat. 'Thank you, Jamie.' This time when she pulled him into a hug, he submitted to her caress without protest.

'Now Grams,' he said excitedly, when at last Sam released him. 'Open Nate's first.' Jamie swiftly passed his great-grandmother a tiny box wrapped in dancing elf paper.

Sam glanced at her boss in surprise.

'Just a little something,' Nate murmured.

Ruby opened her gift slowly, with many pauses to guess what could be inside.

'Just rip it,' Jamie begged, his gaze glued to the package.

'This paper's too pretty to just rip and throw away.' Ruby folded the wrapping and placed it in her bedside drawer.

'Oh!' she exclaimed. Carefully, she lifted a batiked cloth bag from the small box inside. She loosened the bag's drawstring and poured the contents into her hand. 'They're wonderful!' she exclaimed, her eyes lighting up.

'What are they?' Sam asked, leaning

forward to look.

'Magnetized bingo chips,' Ruby said, her voice filled with satisfaction. 'You take this little rod — ' She pulled a stick from the bag. ' — and sweep it across the chips when the game's finished. It picks up all the chips and clears the card for the next game.' She smiled hugely at Nate. 'Thank you,' she said. 'These are just what I needed.'

'What about me?' Jamie asked, gazing at Nate hopefully.

'Jamie!' Sam protested.

With a chuckle, Nate held out a present for Jamie, placing the one intended for Sam into the pocket of his dressing gown.

Jamie eagerly tore his package open. 'Wow!' he exclaimed, extracting a rounded tube from a box. Then he frowned. 'What is it?' he finally asked, turning it over in his hand.

'A kaleidoscope,' Sam cried. She turned to Nate with delight. 'I haven't seen one in years.'

'It was my uncle's,' Nate replied. 'I

172

thought Jamie would like it.'

'Your uncle's!' She frowned. 'Then it's old, probably valuable. Perhaps you shouldn't give it to Jamie,' she said, envisioning her son breaking it in a too enthusiastic twisting of its end.

'He won't break it,' Nate said. 'Will you, Jamie?'

'Of course not!' he said indignantly. 'How does it work?'

Nate took the kaleidoscope from him and held it to his own eye. He trained it on Sam. 'You twist its end, and whatever you're looking at will change shape and colour.'

'Cool!' Jamie exclaimed, taking the toy back. He stared through it at his mother, also. 'Your head's purple and yellow, Mom!' he crowed.

'Let's see how you look,' Sam said with a smile. She held out her hand for the toy.

'Not yet,' Jamie protested. 'Open Nate's present first.'

Slowly, Nate pulled her gift from his pocket.

She reluctantly took it, being careful this time not to touch Nate when she did so. Her fingers fumbled with the wrapping.

'What is it?' she asked nervously, struggling with the last of the tape.

'Open it and see.'

'You shouldn't have got me anything.'

'Why not?' He met her gaze directly, his eyes deep and serious. 'That's what people do at Christmas.'

'Well yes, but . . . it's not what you do. You don't do Christmas at all.'

'I do this year.'

Running her tongue over her bottom lip, Sam ripped the last of the paper. For a long moment, she stared uncomprehendingly at the jewellery box inside then slowly lifted the lid. Her breath caught.

An exquisite heart lay within, a fiery opal in the center of a golden bed and flanking its two sides were an aquamarine and emerald.

'Do you like it?' he asked softly.

'It's beautiful,' she whispered, entranced by the delicate design and the glitter of gemstones.

'May I see?' her grandmother asked, rising from her chair. She lifted the ornament from its bed by a lacy gold chain. 'How wonderful!' she breathed, glancing swiftly at Sam. 'These are our birthstones,' she explained, pointing to the gems.

Sam frowned.

Ruby touched the opal with the tip of her finger. 'The heart is yours, Sam, here in the middle, and this is Jamie's emerald and my aquamarine.' She beamed at Nate. 'It's like a family ring, only this one's a necklace.'

'Family,' Sam whispered. She took a deep breath. When she'd first seen the box, she had thought it contained a ring.

An engagement ring.

For her.

All this talk of marriage and weddings was crazy-making.

'Thank you,' she said, pushing her

fantasies from her mind. She couldn't imagine what it cost Nate emotionally to give her this necklace, to think of her family while his own family was dead.

'Thank you,' she said again, whispering it this time. Words seemed inadequate to convey the emotion she felt then. She stared into Nate's eyes and knew he understood.

'You're welcome,' he answered huskily. 'Here — ' He took the necklace from Ruby's hand and moved around behind Sam. ' — let me help you.'

She shivered the instant his fingers touched her neck. Then he lifted her hair and her goose bumps spread. He draped the necklace around her neck and it fell to just above her breasts, resting there as though she'd never been without it.

His fingers lingered on the clasp a second longer than necessary, and with heightened awareness, she knew she didn't want them to leave, didn't want to lose this connection of skin to skin, heat to heat.

She forced herself to turn. 'I have something for you too.'

'There's nothing I need.'

'You need a lot of things.' She managed a shaky smile.

'Giving up your Christmas plans to come on this cruise was gift enough.'

Sam glanced around the cabin filled with Christmas warmth, at the tree Nate had produced, at the wrapping paper decorating the floor, and finally, lingeringly at the necklace around her neck.

'We've given up nothing.' She hadn't wanted to come, hadn't wanted to spend time in such close proximity to Nate, but now she was glad she had.

And in the next instant she felt completely terrified.

'Excuse me,' she stammered, swallowing hard and backing up. She moved hastily from Jamie's cabin to her own, and for a long moment gazed into her dressing table mirror. The necklace Nate had given her glistened back at her from the glass, looking as wonderful around her neck as it had in the box. Everywhere she went now, she'd be carrying her loved ones with her.

Nate had given that to her.

She swiped her hand across her eyes and removed the moisture welling there, then went to her closet and pulled out a rolled-up canvas. Tucking it under one arm, she returned to the others.

'This is for you,' she said, handing the roll to Nate. 'Merry Christmas.'

He took it from her slowly, and just as slowly unrolled it. Butterflies, vivid as tropical blooms, seemed to fly off the canvas.

'Technically, it's not very accurate,' Sam apologised, but she found herself examining the picture now with as much pleasure as she had when she'd first spotted it in a gallery window. 'The Tiger Butterflies are mixed in with — '

'They're beautiful,' Nate said hoarsely.

'I thought for your wall at home,'

Sam went on hurriedly, feeling suddenly shy beneath the intensity of his gaze. 'Not that I think — '

'I know exactly what you think.' He gave her a rueful smile. 'You made that perfectly clear when you visited me.'

'Well — ' She searched for words that wouldn't offend. ' — your walls could use a little colour.'

'This picture should do the trick.' He shook his head. 'I don't know how you managed to find anything like this.'

Warmth filled her veins clear down to her toes.

'Even with technical imperfections,' he went on, 'it's perfect.' With a startling suddenness, he leaned forward and kissed her cheek.

She was suddenly filled with a need for more, to feel his lips on hers, and his hands on her body. A need she couldn't admit to. She pushed Nate away and glanced dazedly toward her grandmother and Jamie.

Ruby was watching them, a pleased smile on her lips, but Jamie, thank heavens, was engrossed in his new toy.

'Breakfast?' Sam suggested.

* * *

Sam wrenched her arm around and attempted to rub the sunscreen onto the small of her back, keeping, as she did so, her gaze averted from Nate. She didn't want to look at him lying on the deck chair next to her, didn't want to see his long legs, already turning brown, stretched so close to her own. Or his broad chest, either, much more muscular when naked than she had expected from seeing him clothed.

'Need some help?' Nate asked, in a lazy voice.

'I'm fine.' But in the next instant she felt his hand on her back, caressing her skin in an upward motion.

'Stop!' She struggled to sit up. 'What are you doing?'

'Catching a drip,' he replied, not stopping the movement of his hand.

'Relax, or you'll get lotion all over your bathing suit.'

She tried to relax, tried to ease back onto her chair. Anything more was beyond her capabilities. For his touch created spirals of sensation that began on her skin's surface then immediately sank deeper. It didn't help to know he was watching her as he rubbed, was growing intimately familiar with every exposed inch of her body.

'You're beginning to burn,' he said disapprovingly.

'I never burn.'

'Maybe not in Seattle, but you've been lying in that position since you got on deck.'

'It's only been a couple of minutes.' She didn't want to turn over, for if she did she'd be facing him, and no matter how much she told herself she didn't care, she didn't look like the younger women sprawled out along the deck, no longer had the concave belly she'd possessed before giving birth.

'It's been half an hour at least.'

Propping herself onto her elbows, Sam risked a glance over her shoulder. Nate was examining her back as though she had the plague.

'Turn over,' he ordered, 'before I do it for you. I'll do your stomach,' he added.

'That's not necessary,' she muttered, but she could feel the sun's heat now across the top of her shoulders, and its touch was laced with fire.

It wasn't just her stomach stopping her from facing Nate. If she rolled over she was liable to fall out of her bathing suit altogether, the one her friend Cheryl had convinced her to buy. It would attract the men, her friend had insisted when Sam had dubiously eyed it in the store's full-length mirror.

What kind of men? Sam had demanded, tugging the legs down and the bra up.

The fun kind, Cheryl had assured her.

Nate? Sam wondered, glancing worriedly at her boss. There was already chemistry between them that would do neither any good. To parade in front of him like a centrefold in a men's magazine would send the wrong message.

Probably already had.

She'd insisted last night they keep their distance from each other, yet this morning he had kissed her. And now here he was with his hands on her naked flesh.

With a frustrated sigh, she thrust from her mind how good it felt and swiftly rolled over, moving so suddenly his hand became caught in the space between her body and the chair.

'Sorry,' she mumbled, her face as hot now as her shoulders and back. She lifted her buttocks and he pulled his hand free.

'No problem,' he replied, drawing a finger across her bare belly.

'Hey! I said I'd do the rest myself.'

'Excess lotion,' he explained, holding up cream-smeared fingers.

Sitting up altogether, she grabbed the

lotion from the table between them and squeezed some onto her own palm. With quick efficient movements, she swabbed it swiftly onto her chest and neck. Then down her arms, belly and legs, keeping, all the while, her shoulders as straight as possible.

'You missed a spot,' Nate said, pointing to an area above her left breast.

Lest he harbour any ideas of covering the area for her, Sam swiftly dabbed on more lotion.

'You could do me now,' Nate suggested, rolling over onto his tummy.

'What?'

'A little of that cream would feel good.' He gestured lazily toward his back.

Stiffly, reluctantly, Sam dabbed some cream onto his shoulder. His body felt even warmer than hers, as though his inner temperature was set at a steady five degrees higher. Or maybe it was nerves chilling her skin, or the sudden desire flaring through her to caress him more intimately.

With a hard swallow, she streaked the lotion the length of his back then smeared it around in a couple of swift strokes.

'Hey,' said a voice from behind. 'That's not the way to do it.'

Sam turned and peered against the blinding sun.

'You're going to grind that stuff right through the poor man's pores!' Fay protested, stepping around to Nate's other side. 'You're supposed to massage it in.' She took the lotion from Sam's hand. 'Like this.' Bestowing a sultry smile on Nate, she squeezed a dot of the cream onto her palm then gently, sensuously, rubbed it onto his back.

Sam picked up her blouse from the back of her lounger and hastily drew it on, not feeling better until she had buttoned the last button. Maybe now she could stop worrying about how she looked in her bikini, could stop feeling like a sixteen-year-old with adult desires. Especially as Fay had somehow managed, with an artful arrangement of webbing and lace, to look sexier in her one-piece than any other woman on the deck.

Sam caught her cheek between her teeth and watched Fay slowly work her hands down Nate's back. She should be relieved the other woman had taken over, should be glad to no longer share the intimacy of Nate's touch, but for some reason she didn't. Fighting off the urge to snatch the lotion back, she picked up, instead, her bottle of water.

'Feels good,' Nate murmured drowsily.

Gritting her teeth, Sam subdued the desire to tip the liquid over Nate's head.

As contentedly as a ginger cat basking in the sun, Fay hummed as her hands drifted lower. She lifted the waistband of Nate's trunks and rubbed the lotion an inch beneath it, then back up his sides, which, from where Sam sat seething, appeared to be in shadow.

When Fay started in on the tops of his legs, Sam could stand it no longer.

'I'm going to find Jamie and Grams,' she said, rising. 'I haven't seen them since lunch.'

'Jamie's with the kids' club counsellor and Ruby's playing bingo,' Nate murmured, not bothering to lift his head.

'Oh,' Sam said crossly, irritated he knew more than she about where her family was and what they were doing.

'They came looking for you when you went to collect your book from the cabin. They said they'd meet you here later.'

'So when were you planning on telling me this?'

'I'm telling you now.' He glanced up at her for an instant then turned his attention back to Fay, who was now sitting on the edge of his lounger working the backs of his legs.

'You should be a professional,' he said appreciatively to the redhaired woman.

'I've been trained by the best,' Fay answered. 'Learning how to massage was the only thing I got from my first husband that didn't have a price tag attached.'

'Worth a king's ransom,' Nate purred.

Sam banged her water bottle down. 'Tell Grams and Jamie I'll be in my room.' She turned to move away.

'Jamie said something about a table tennis competition.' Nate glanced lazily at his watch. 'It should be starting soon.'

Sam looked to where the table tennis tables lay tucked out of the wind between two out-jutting storage rooms. The kids' club leader was already there, taking out paddles and balls, and writing names in chalk on a board.

With a sigh, Sam sank back onto her lounger. 'You seem to be in the know,' she muttered at Nate.

'Timing is everything,' he responded cheerfully. 'Can I get either of you a drink?'

'Nothing for me,' Sam said.

'Champagne,' Fay replied, lifting her arm to push a strand of hair from her eyes. With the movement, her bathing suit pulled tautly over firm breasts, and well-toned muscles sculpted each arm.

Fitness club, Sam decided dismally, scowling at her own rounded and definitely un-toned arms. Fay obviously had the time, money, and no lifelong addiction to chocolate to undermine her efforts.

Is that what she'd let herself in for on this cruise? Comparisons with women against whom she could never compete? Against whom she didn't want to compete, she reminded herself crossly. Which was another reason to marry off Nate Robbins as swiftly as possible. Perhaps then the infatuation she'd acquired for the man would disappear and she could stop examining every woman she met with an eye that ended up trained critically on her own self.

'Mom!' Jamie called.

Sam twisted in the direction of her

son's voice, and saw him wading through a sea of deckchairs towards her. Her smile of welcome faded when she saw the distress on his face.

'What's the matter?' she asked, leaning forward to catch him as he hurtled the last two yards and landed in her arms. 'Why aren't you getting ready for the table tennis match?'

'I can't play,' he said bleakly. His mouth drooped another notch.

'Why not? You know how. You spent hours playing it at day camp last summer.'

'It's not that.' His eyes brimmed with moisture. 'It's a pairs' match today.'

'Well, I'm no world champ, but I can hit a ball. I'll play with you.'

'You can't.' A tear trickled down Jamie's cheek. With an angry swipe, he brushed it away. 'It's a father and son match, and I don't have a father.'

For the millionth time since her husband had deserted them, Sam silently cursed Phil's name. If he could see the pain etched on his son's face and curved into the slump of his shoulders, he never could have left. With a sigh, she pulled Jamie closer.

'If you don't mind a stand-in, I'd be honored to play with you,' Nate offered softly.

Sam glanced at him over her son's shoulder and saw the same anger in Nate's eyes she knew was in her own.

'Really?' Jamie asked, tugging loose from Sam and twisting to face Nate.

'I was two-time champion my eighth grade year,' Nate replied with a grin.

'Mom?' Jamie asked, whirling back to Sam, his face alight now with hope.

'Go for it,' she said. Her heart soared with gratitude. 'Thank you,' she mouthed to Nate.

Jamie's face suddenly sobered. 'What if they don't let Nate play?' He bit his lower lip and glanced in the direction of the play leader.

'Of course they will,' Sam said gently. 'I bet half the kids here don't have their real dads playing with them.'

'Maybe you're right,' her son said

slowly. 'I met two boys this morning who are travelling with their uncle, and another kid who said his mom's boyfriend was worse than hopeless, but was better than nothing.' Jamie's face brightened. 'Nate could be that, couldn't he, Mom?'

Sam froze.

'Be your boyfriend, I mean,' her child explained patiently.

'I don't think we have to go that far,' Sam choked out, cursing the heat searing her neck and cheeks.

'Great idea, Jamie,' Nate said, rising from his lounger. 'Let's go practise.'

Before she could say more, they were walking away together, Nate's hand on Jamie's shoulder and the boy's head inclined towards him as he chattered.

'Now there's a man a woman could fall for,' Fay said thoughtfully.

'You think so?' Sam replied.

'Definitely.' She glanced at Sam. 'From the look on your face, I'd say you already have.'

'You're wrong.'

Fay's brows lifted.

'He's my boss, nothing more.'

'He's handsome, charming, wealthy — '

'He's not wealthy,' Sam denied.

One look in Fay's direction told Sam the classmate didn't believe her. Which was probably a good thing. She was supposed to be marrying Nate off, not spoiling his chances with an eligible woman.

Fay twirled the diamond earring piercing her lobe. 'So you won't mind if I go after him myself?' she asked.

'No . . . ' Sam replied, fighting off the sudden urge to reply that she did. Nate's plan, until now, had seemed ridiculous and impossible, involving unnamed women with unidentified agendas, but in the beat of a heart everything had changed.

Fay was not some stranger Sam could convince herself would be good for Nate, would be good to him, no matter how ridiculous were his ideas. Fay's view of marriage was as lacking in love and respect as Nate's, but while

Sam suspected Nate's ideas were born of despair, Fay's seemed to stem from avarice.

Fay would eat Nate alive, and he wouldn't even know it until she had chewed him up and spat him out.

Sam glanced to where Nate and Jamie were batting the ball. Her son was animated and laughing, was giggling so uncontrollably at whatever Nate was saying that his serve skewed wildly off and buried the ball in the carefully coiffed hair of a woman reading through pointed tortoiseshell sunglasses.

Raising a finger to his lips to quiet Sam's horrified son, Nate tiptoed up behind the woman and without her even noticing, plucked the ball from her hair. Which feat reduced Jamie to another spasm of giggles.

Sam couldn't stop a smile from creeping across her own face. Nate was wonderful with her son, would make a terrific father one day if he would only allow himself to take the chance, if he would marry someone with whom he could fall in love, and who would love him in return. That someone was not a woman like Fay.

'I don't mind in the slightest,' she lied, turning back to Fay, 'but Nate's already interested in someone else. They're getting together tomorrow.'

'That's too bad,' Fay replied. She looked at Sam thoughtfully. 'Anyone I know?'

'I wouldn't imagine so.'

'What's her name?'

'Her name?' Sam thought desperately. 'I think he said it was Sharon. Or maybe it was Susan?' She shrugged. 'Something starting with an 'S'.' Her gaze raked the deck and was caught by a striking brunette in a white sundress walking past the hot tub and about to disappear along the starboard side. 'That's her,' she lied, pointing.

'Pretty,' Fay replied.

'Yes,' Sam agreed. Relief coursed through her as the brown-haired woman disappeared from sight.

'When are they meeting?'

Panic swept away the relief. 'Lunch-time,' she strangled out, visualizing her lies multiplying like schools of tropical fish. 'Nate was supposed to be meeting a business colleague, but he postponed that for his lunch date.'

'A man who puts romance first,' Fay said thoughtfully.

'Something like that.'

'Not my kind of man, then. Oh well,' her classmate said, 'there are plenty of other goldfish in the sea.'

'Right,' Sam replied. She could only pray Nate never discovered he'd hooked himself a potential wife, and that Sam had grabbed hold and thrown her back.

# 9

Grams was nowhere to be found. Even Jamie didn't know where his great-grandmother was and Jamie kept track of the old woman at all times. Sam had often seen his anxious gaze glued to Ruby's back, as though he expected her to disappear like his father.

All the books Sam had read on divorce indicated Jamie had been too young to even remember his dad, much less mourn him, but sometimes in his eyes there was a sadness only a father could eradicate.

Like yesterday, when he'd needed a partner for the table tennis match. If Nate hadn't stepped in . . .

She couldn't think about Nate now. She had to find Grams, had to talk to her or someone before she went crazy. And that someone couldn't be Fay as it was her she had lied to.

Sam smoothed the hem of her shorts and fleetingly wondered as she pushed open the door to the shipboard casino, if people were allowed inside dressed for a day at the beach.

She needn't have worried. The man working the nearest slot machine showed more sunburned skin than she could bear to see. She moved further into the darkened room. The sudden chill of the air-conditioning raised goose bumps on her skin. She crossed her arms, tried to make herself warmer. She was wasting her time looking in here. Grams was no doubt ensconced in some cosy nook working away diligently on her latest crossword book.

But if so, why hadn't she been able to find her? It wasn't like Grams to be late, especially as she had promised this morning, when she and Jamie hurried off to an early breakfast, to meet Sam around ten for a cup of herbal tea.

The cards flashing from the croupier's hand to the green velvet of the blackjack table caught Sam's attention.

The players around the table had all settled their features into a mask-like position as they struggled to keep secret the hands they'd been dealt. Except for the blonde woman in a lime-green dress. With a pout of disappointment, she laid her cards down.

Sam twisted her lips in sympathy and pushed her way past the crowd gathered around the roulette table. A tinkling laugh stopped her dead. She turned around and her eyes widened.

With a spot of colour showing high on each cheek, Grams pushed a pile of chips towards the number black forty-four. Next to her stood a straight-backed gentleman sporting a handlebar moustache whose age-spotted hand was tucked securely around her grandmother's waist. It was the man who sat next to Grams each mealtime in the dining room.

'Grams?' Sam cried.

Her grandmother glanced up and smiled.

'What are you doing?' Sam stared

incredulously at her grandmother's chips and tried not to imagine how much she was going to lose.

'Just having a little flutter,' Ruby replied. 'Now shush, dear, they're about to spin.'

Sam gasped in a shallow breath and watched the roulette wheel turn. The ball bounced and jumped, and numbers and colours blended with each other until at last the ball halted on the very number Ruby had chosen.

With a squeal of excitement, her grandmother flung her hands in the air, and then, ignoring Sam, turned and kissed the old gentleman full on the lips.

'Grams!' Sam exclaimed again.

Ruby twisted back and gave Sam a huge hug, then turned to the croupier and watched with dancing eyes as he pushed her winnings towards her with a hoe-shaped stick.

Ruby touched the moustachioed gentleman's hand. 'What do you think, Charles?' she asked. 'Shall I quit now?'

'Whatever you think best, my dear,' he replied in a voice both smooth and southern.

*My dear?* Sam's ears burned. This man was a stranger. Sitting next to her grandmother at dinner didn't entitle him to call her *dear*.

With a gracious smile towards the other players, Ruby swept her chips off the table and into her capacious handbag just as though she'd been doing it every day of her life. The chips showed up blackly against the sea of blue wool from which her grandmother was knitting Sam a sweater.

'We've got to talk,' Sam said sternly. She took hold of her grandmother's arm.

'We're sitting just over there,' Ruby replied, gesturing toward a table nestled up against a window. 'Charles, you remember my granddaughter Sam. Sam, you remember Charles.'

Stiffly, Sam nodded.

'What would you ladies like to drink?' Charles asked.

'A cup of tea,' Sam replied. She

suddenly longed for its potent warmth on the crackling dryness of her throat.

'Another piña colada for me, dear,' her grandmother said.

Sam's mouth fell open. 'It's only ten-thirty in the morning!'

'Iced tea,' Charles asked, 'or herbal?'

'Black and hot,' Sam replied grimly, 'and make it strong.' She waited until Charles had moved out of earshot then turned to her grandmother. 'What on earth's going on?'

'Whatever do you mean?'

'Gambling! Drinking!'

'It's just a little fun.' Ruby's laughter tinkled again. 'We are on holiday after all.'

'Yes, but — ' The last semblance of control seeped from Sam's body. ' — you've never done this before.'

'I've always wanted to.'

Sam's mouth dropped open, but no words came out.

'I've got a system,' Ruby went on, leaning forward in a conspiratorial manner.

'A system?'

'I flip a coin. If it's heads I choose red, and if it's tails I choose black, and then to choose the right number I multiply — '

'Grams!'

'You're right.' Ruby glanced furtively at the surrounding tables. 'I shouldn't be telling you this in here.' She leaned even closer. 'Someone might overhear.'

Sam closed her eyes, but even with them shut it felt as though she were hanging upside down looking out at the world with the cockeyed view of a bat. She'd come to her grandmother for help, knowing her to be sensible, clear-thinking, logical. Not the sort of woman who gambled fistfuls of tokens and drank piña colada's before noon!

Opening her eyes again, she gazed dazedly at her grandmother. She suddenly felt as though she didn't know her, perhaps didn't even want to know her, most certainly didn't want to ask her for advice regarding Nate.

'Now what is it, dear?' Ruby asked.

She couldn't, wouldn't throw her troubles into her grandmother's lap. She had to concentrate instead on getting her family off this boat before they all dissolved completely into madness.

'Is it something about Nate?' Ruby went on.

'Grams,' Sam said uncertainly, 'I don't think we should — '

'What? Now speak up, child. What's the trouble?'

Sam sighed. When her grandmother spoke in that tone it was impossible not to tell her what she demanded to know. 'I've told someone something that isn't exactly the truth — '

'Never lie,' her grandmother said firmly. 'Lies have a way of biting you on the bum.'

'This one already has.' With another sigh, she capitulated, desperate now to explain before Charles got back with the drinks. 'Fay was showing an interest in Nate.'

'A romantic interest?'

'Yes.'

'And you didn't like that?'

'I just don't think Fay's the right woman for Nate.'

'I thought you didn't care who he married.'

'I don't care,' Sam said sharply. A throbbing began at her temples. 'It's just that I know Fay. She would make him miserable. Nate might have some nutty ideas on marriage but he's otherwise a nice guy.'

'Very nice,' her grandmother agreed.

'But whether Fay likes him or not is not my difficulty. I — ' She bit her lip, tried to find the right words. 'I told Fay that Nate had a lunch date today.'

'And he doesn't?'

'No.' She swallowed hard. 'I also told her who he had the date with.'

'And who is the lucky lady?' Ruby's lips twitched.

The sick feeling intensified in the pit of Sam's stomach. 'I saw a woman walking by on the deck and told Fay it was her.' She propped her head on her hands, and groaned. 'I don't even know her name.'

'But you know what she looks like?'

'Yes.'

'Then the solution's simple. Find her, invite her to lunch, and make sure Nate's there.'

Sam lifted her head and glanced at her grandmother gratefully. 'That could work,' she said slowly.

'Of course it could,' Ruby said. 'Now here's Charlie. We'll have a nice drink together and then you can — '

'Can't do that now, Grams,' Sam said hastily. She rose from her chair, and in the process almost knocked Charlie into her grandmother's lap. 'I've got to go and find that woman.'

★ ★ ★

Easier said than done. Sam was beginning to feel she knew this ship even better than Jamie, who explored it relentlessly from dawn 'til dusk.

If anyone had asked her two weeks

prior how she'd be spending Boxing Day, she would have answered contentedly that she'd be sitting in her overstuffed chair at home warming her feet against a slow burning fire, a glass of eggnog in one hand, a good book in the other, and a muffin-sized butter tart on a plate beside her.

She would never have envisioned this frenzied scrambling from bow to stern examining each body laid out in the sun. With the sort of tan the brown-haired woman possessed, she hadn't looked the type to spend a tropical cruise indoors. Desperately, Sam had peered into libraries and poked into the ship's myriad bars and coffee cafés. She had even checked out the gym, pretending an interest in the Stair-Master she didn't really feel.

But she'd had no luck.

Sinking into a lounger next to the pool, Sam flipped her sunglasses over her eyes and held a damp napkin against her perspiring brow. A cold drink of water was what she needed to push away the fog clogging her brain and allow her to determine what to do next.

She raised a hand to signal the waiter, but yanked it down again when two tanned hands topped with scarlet nails gripped the pool edge next to her chair. The brunette for whom she'd been searching pulled herself from the water.

'It's you!' Sam exclaimed.

'I beg your pardon?'

'I've been looking for you.'

'Do I know you?' the woman asked politely, carrying on with the task of towelling her body dry.

'No,' Sam replied, 'but I've been looking for you nonetheless.'

The woman frowned.

'You've won a prize,' Sam explained, ignoring her grandmother's advice about never telling a lie.

'What on earth — '

'The grand prize,' Sam continued. 'I work for a toy company — '

The woman stared at her, puzzled.

' — and our marketing people decided that as my boss was booked for this cruise, it would be a great promotional idea to give away free toys in a big draw. Because it's Christmas!' Sam added brightly, hoping those magical words would dispel the suspicion replacing the confusion in the woman's eyes.

'Christmas is over and . . . I didn't enter any draw.' The woman continued to frown as she turbaned her towel around her head. 'And I don't need any toys.'

'It's not just toys you win, Miss . . . er . . . Miss — ' She reached into her pocket and pulled out the receipt she'd received when she had purchased her sunglasses from the ship's boutique. She made a show of smoothing it open.

'Vivian Clare,' the woman supplied, giving her towel an impatient twist.

'Vivian . . . of course.' Sam hastily put her receipt away. 'As I was saying, you also win a free morning at the ship's beauty spa. Whatever you want done — ' She gestured with widespread palms. ' — it's yours.'

'Well,' Vivian said, 'I've already booked a mud bath for this morning.' She pulled her watch from the gaily coloured raffia bag sitting on the deck and checked the time. 'Oh Lord,' she cried in dismay, 'I'm late.'

'Take your time,' Sam said grandly, praying she could get to the phone before Vivian got to the spa. 'Robbins' Toys will pick up the tab.'

'Well!' the woman exclaimed. Her face grew more amiable. 'That sounds fine.'

'When you've finished at the spa,' Sam went on, 'my boss has invited you to lunch in San Juan. At the exclusive Cabana Resort.' She winced at the doubt reappearing in the brunette's eyes. 'Publicity photos, champagne, the toys,' she explained brightly. 'And did I mention the hundred dollar gift certificate? They say the shopping in Puerto Rico is fantastic.'

'Shopping!' The woman's dubious

look disappeared. 'Fine. I'll be there.'

'A cab will be waiting by the dock at two.'

★ ★ ★

Sam lifted her face to the sun and felt its heat ease the tension digging grooves into her forehead. Vivian would be here any minute. The driver had been instructed to take her the scenic way around, past the Fort on the top of the hill then back down through the shopper-thronged streets to the road following the curve of the shoreline.

Everything had been organized in haste, and had cost more money than Sam wanted to consider. But she'd managed it. She'd phoned the ship's spa and arranged for Vivian's mud bath to be billed to Nate, had also ordered champagne and roses to be placed in Vivian's bedroom along with a card as to shuttle boat times and taxis. Then she had tackled the hardest task of all.

Telling Nate he had a date.

211

The news hadn't thrilled him. In fact, when she'd added that it would cost him in the neighbourhood of five hundred dollars, he'd scowled at her so fiercely she became convinced his face would be permanently tangled.

He'd even growled that he had no intention of paying that kind of money to date some woman he didn't know. Sam had snapped back that if he was going to maintain that sort of attitude he might as well give up now.

She placed her fingertips on her temples and rubbed in a circular fashion. The dull ache that had plagued her all morning was now a piercing pain, had been intensifying since she'd bumped into Fay outside the ship's gift shop.

Fay had asked the time of Nate's lunch date as she wanted to invite him for a drink later, leaving Sam in no doubt that Fay had decided after all that Nate was her kind of man.

Under a pressure of lies growing too great to bear, Sam had babbled out the whole story of Nate lunching late as his date — Vivian being her name, not Susan or Sharon — had a spa appointment in the morning. Sam had mentioned, also, that she wasn't sure what they'd be doing after that, but had implied the date might go on, and on, and on.

Fay's lips had tightened, and she had murmured if that was the case, she might as well take the city bus tour of San Juan. At which point she left as the bus departed from the dock in forty-five minutes.

Sam wished *she* could play tourist and go on a bus tour, or that she'd accepted Gram's invitation to accompany her, Charlie, and Jamie on a tour of the old Fort. Perhaps history and military strategies would succeed in banishing the morning from her mind, would clarify her options should Nate fail to marry on time.

One thing was for certain, she'd have to find another job, for if Robbins' Toys survived at all, it was in for a major downsizing. Nate would no longer be able to afford the wage she needed to keep her household going, and she couldn't bear to watch everything Nate cared for disappear.

With a sigh, Sam twisted her wrist to elude the sun's glare and glanced at her watch.

It was already two-thirty.

Vivian was late.

If she took any longer, Nate would come storming out of that restaurant like a newly-released bull. When she'd left him a half hour prior, he was already drumming his fingers on the starched linen table cloth, and his lips were pressed together and his eyes crossly narrowed. When the wine steward had approached, he'd all but bitten off the man's head.

There was the taxi now. Sam let out her breath in a single rush and, with the tiniest of movements, pressed her body flat against the stone back of the bench. She'd positioned herself far enough from the entrance that Vivian wouldn't see her, but close enough to afford a view of the other woman's arrival. Once she was in the restaurant, Sam could safely leave.

The doorman opened the cab's door and slender, silk-clad legs emerged. But the body following the legs didn't belong to Vivian. This woman was blonde, with a head of tight curls and a toddler by the hand.

Sam's heart sank. She had no choice now. She would have to face Nate herself and somehow convince him that Vivian was still coming.

Reluctantly, she stood and followed the path to the entrance. Her feet moved as though glued to the white pebbles beneath, but her mind raced, formulating, then discarding, first one plan then the next.

\* \* \*

'This isn't necessary,' Sam muttered.

'We have to eat,' Nate replied. He speared a prawn with his fork and dipped it into a bowl of spicy red sauce.

'I thought you'd be upset.'

'I never liked blind dates.'

'She might show up yet.'

'Then we'll pull up an extra chair.'

'If you didn't want a date,' Sam asked tersely, 'why ask me to get you one?'

'God knows,' Nate said cheerfully. He popped the prawn into his mouth. 'Do you want me to be upset?'

'I want you to care. Time's running out.'

'I've stopped looking at the calendar.' Nate glanced at the sunshine glittering off the turquoise surf and splashing in the picture window at them. 'It must be the weather.'

'It's *your* marriage! *Your* wife! You've got to take some interest! You can't leave it all up to me.'

'It's not my job, *mon*,' Nate replied, intoning the phrase scrawled across the tee shirts in the market.

'Your business is!' Sam said sharply. 'Are you willing to let that fall apart from lack of trying?'

'Relax.' Nate stabbed a scallop next from the seafood platter and moved it toward her mouth. 'Open wide,' he instructed, holding his other hand beneath her chin to catch the butter dribbling from the delicacy.

'I don't want — ' Too late. The morsel was already past her lips and landing on her tongue in an explosion of taste sensation.

'Good?' he asked, his hand poised to repeat the process.

'Good,' she admitted, but covered his hand with hers, determined to stop its upward movement before he could touch her again, before her body could react as it had before, with a spiralling rush of heat and heightened senses.

Perhaps she had simply sat too long in the sun, or drunk too swiftly of the excellent Chardonnay, but Sam suddenly felt relaxed, more relaxed than she'd felt since beginning this voyage, so relaxed, in fact, that it bordered on out of control.

She tried to sit straighter, tried to draw away from Nate's reach, but given her swiftly vanishing resolve and the intimacy of their window alcove, she found the task impossible.

Nate seemed to feel what was passing between them also, for he suddenly raised his hand and motioned for the check. When he turned back to her, his eyes were serious.

'So what's next?' he asked. 'Shall we go back to the boat or scour the city for my so-called date?'

'What do you want to do?'

'I want to forget the whole thing.'

'We can't,' she said miserably.

'No. But we're not going to miss out on seeing San Juan just because some woman decides to stand me up.'

'I'm sure — '

He abruptly stood and pulled out her chair. 'Come on,' he said, throwing some bills on the table. 'There's something I want to show you.'

\* \* \*

'Well!' Grams exclaimed. 'Just look at you!'

'What do you mean?' Sam plopped into the chair by her grandmother's window, and wished she could open it and cool her face on the sea breeze.

'Bright eyes, flushed skin — '

Sam flinched.

'You look like a woman who's — '

'Grams!' Sam protested.

' — fallen in love,' her grandmother finished. Then she turned back to her knitting as though this pronouncement was the most natural thing in the world.

'I'm not in love,' Sam denied, but her heart began to soar.

'So how is Nate?' her grandmother asked.

'Fine.' Sam averted her face, couldn't bear her grandmother's scrutiny.

'How did his date go?'

'It didn't.'

'He didn't like the woman?'

'She didn't show up.'

'Hm.'

Sam shot her grandmother a glance,

saw her attempt nonchalance as she picked up the stitch she had dropped in her knitting. 'You knew,' Sam accused.

'I guessed,' Ruby admitted. Her needles clicked furiously.

'But how — '

'I saw that Vivian Clare woman when I went down for my hair appointment.'

With a start, Sam realized her grandmother's hair was no longer caught up in the bun she usually wore. How could she have missed the transformation to this stylish cut, to this artful mingling of white hair with grey, interspersed with a highlighted suggestion of silver?

Why hadn't she noticed it the instant she entered the room? Had she been so caught up in her own worries she hadn't really looked at her own grandmother?

'It looks wonderful,' she said now, 'though it makes you look — '

'Go on,' her grandmother urged.

' — like a stranger,' Sam finished. 'An elegant stranger,' she added hastily.

Although her grandmother's eyes were the same, and they were looking at her now with the same warmth as always. 'What made you decide to get it cut?'

A splash of red on her grandmother's bedside table suddenly caught Sam's eye. 'Oh,' she finished lamely, taking in the roses. 'It was that man you were with . . . Charlie.'

It was her grandmother's turn to flush. 'I've been thinking for a while I needed to spruce myself up.' Her cheeks turned a deeper pink. 'This seemed as good a time as any.'

'You've always looked wonderful, Grams.'

'A person has to keep up with the times.'

'Have you been unhappy?' Sam asked worriedly.

'Unhappy? Me?' Her grandmother chuckled. 'Never!' She brushed her hair back from her face in a strangely vulnerable gesture. 'It was simply time to treat my hair as something more than a head warmer. It was my best feature when I was younger.'

'I've always loved your hair.' Sam looked at her grandmother's new coiffure with a pang of regret. 'When you combed it out, it was long enough to sit on.'

'Which was a pain,' her grandmother said firmly. 'It was hard to wash, hard to comb. I wanted something shorter.' She knit another three stitches then came to the end of the row. 'I've been thinking of taking up swimming again.'

'Swimming!'

'I used to be able to swim two miles across a lake — '

'In the dead of winter,' Sam finished for her, 'with the surface freezing over.'

'Don't tease me, girl. I might have been younger then, but there's no reason I can't get that good again. I was thinking Jamie and I could go to the pool together after school some days, and that's not something I want to do with long hair.'

'Are you sure Charlie has nothing to do with this?'

'Charlie liked my hair the way it was.' Ruby gazed at Sam sternly. 'You can't do everything just to please a man! Besides — ' She ran her hand over her silver-streaked head. ' — Charlie said I could be bald as an egg for all he cares.'

'Sounds like the two of you are getting close.'

'Don't look so worried. He's a very nice man.'

'You barely know him.'

'He makes me laugh.' Her grandmother's eyes turned dreamy. 'Besides — ' She leaned closer. ' — he kisses as good as your grandfather.'

'Grams!'

A tinkling laugh erupted from her grandmother's newly reddened lips. 'Don't look so shocked.' Her eyes narrowed. 'It's obvious you've been doing your own share of kissing!'

'I haven't!' Not actually kissed. Not this time. Not on their date that was not a date.

It had almost happened at the Fort. They'd stood together against the stone wall overlooking the ocean. Ghosts of long-ago women seemed to touch Sam, their faces turned to the sea, searching for the ships that would bring their men home.

Nate had turned to her, the tang of his aftershave blanketing her with need, but what had gripped her most was the expression in his eyes: of desire, and want, and a piercing admiration.

She'd leaned towards him, too, unable to resist, and imagined clearly the touch of his lips on hers. But just when she'd decided to give in to her own desires, to allow her heart to lead and ignore her head, Nate had drawn back. Had sucked in a breath so deep and long it was almost as though he were saving himself from drowning.

When he pulled away, it was as though a cloud had covered the sun, and with the loss of its warmth, the moment lost its glory.

Sam touched her lips with her tongue, felt on them still the anticipated taste of Nate. With a shiver, she turned back to her grandmother.

'You saw Vivian?' she prompted, needing a diversion from this talk of Nate.

'She could scarcely walk, poor thing,' her grandmother said. 'And the girl from the spa was as red as a cherry. Kept saying sorry and telling her that the next visit would be free.' Grams shook her head. 'Your Miss Clare — '

'She's not *my* Miss Clare.'

' — told her sharply that this visit was free, for all the good it had done her. The beautician looked even more miserable than before and offered her the works next time.'

'What on earth happened?'

'They forgot her in the mud bath.' Ruby shook her head. 'Not a good thing, I understand. Once you're in that bath you can't get out again without help.' She shuddered. 'I don't understand the appeal myself. If the good Lord intended us to wallow in the mud, he'd have made us pigs.'

'It's supposed to deep clean your

pores,' Sam explained, with a chuckle, 'as well as be relaxing.'

'It was a little too relaxing from the look of Vivian Clare.' Ruby grimaced. 'The poor woman's knees buckled. They had to call a steward to help her to her room.'

'No wonder she didn't turn up for lunch!'

'Your friend Fay was in the spa as well. Making appointments to treat herself royally.' Ruby shot Sam a smug smile. 'But she didn't spend the afternoon with a handsome man either!'

'He's my boss, Grams.'

'All the better.' Ruby patted her on the knee. 'You've got time and proximity to get to know him.'

'Time? There's no time!'

'Your grandfather and I fell in love the instant we met.'

'I told you before, Nate doesn't believe in love.' Although she, too, had felt the barb of Cupid's arrow when they'd met. For months she had tried to deny the attraction, for she needed her job, couldn't afford an office romance. To say nothing of the fact Nate had never seemed to notice her.

'Nate doesn't know what he believes,' her grandmother said firmly. 'He has to feel love first to truly believe in it.'

'He's already done that once.'

'Then he's capable of it again.'

# 10

He had almost kissed her. It was all he could do not to look at her now. If he'd known what would happen up at the Fort, he never would have taken her there, never would have trusted himself alone with her.

Never would have booked this snorkeling trip for today. But he hadn't had the heart to cancel it, not after seeing her face that first day on board, when they'd poured through the itinerary of ship's tours and activities and had spotted the snorkeling and scuba trips available. When he told her he'd booked places for the two of them and Jamie, the light in her eyes had melted his defences.

She wasn't smiling now. Sam was staring at the water lapping her toes as expressionlessly as a con artist, and when she glanced in his direction, she just as swiftly averted her gaze.

The only time she smiled was when she looked at Jamie. The boy, at least, was enjoying himself. Warmth settled in Nate's chest. Sam's son was great.

Sam turned her back to the sea and placed her mask over her head, rendering her face dwarfed by the snorkel. She took firm hold of Jamie's hand as they edged backward through the soft sand, that being the only way to move with flippers on their feet.

Despite the snorkeling apparel, Sam still looked gorgeous. Her bathing suit hugged her form, delineating her shape in sharp detail. Tendrils of her hair snaked down her cheeks and neck from the knot on the top of her head.

But it was the way she bent toward her child and helped Jamie move in his cumbersome footwear that really tugged at Nate's heart.

He slipped his mask over his eyes and slipped into the ocean also. Hopefully immersion in cold water would arrest the need he felt every time he looked at Sam.

But the Caribbean Sea was not nearly cold enough to stop the heat. The water's warmth was as sensuous as silk, and it curled around his body as sinuously as a woman.

This desire had to stop. He couldn't marry Sam. Not if he wanted to stick to his plan.

Clamping his teeth on his snorkel, Nate thrust his head under. In the distance he could see Sam and Jamie swimming slowly along the shoreline. Schools of tropical fish flitted and streaked across their path, while other fish swam sedately alongside them, no doubt waiting for the fish food clutched in Jamie's hand.

Despite his determination, Nate smiled again, and this time paid for the gesture with a rush of water into his mouth. He quickly surfaced and spit it out, blowing through his snorkel to clear the tube.

He scanned the surface to where he'd

last seen Sam and Jamie, and found them farther down the beach than he'd have thought possible in the short time they'd been swimming, and further out than he thought safe. They were almost to the pilings of a crumbling pier that stretched out into the ocean where the sandy beach ended and the rocks began.

Jamie had gone farther than Sam. He was almost to the pier while she swam in a lazy circle as though following a fish intent on tying her in knots.

Nate's brows drew together. Where the hell was the kid going? He'd reached the pilings now and had disappeared beneath them. Nate snapped his mask back over his face and dove.

He tried to still the urgency driving him to swim swiftly, tried to quiet the sudden pounding of his heart with the measured stroke of his arms, tried not to think what might be lurking in the cooler waters beneath the wharf.

His flippers propelled him faster than

he'd ever swum before. He could see Sam now to his right, her body straight up and down as she broke the surface of the water. She was twisting and turning as though trying to get her bearings, and Nate knew in his gut that she was looking for Jamie.

He pressed harder, driving his arms through the water in a desperate attempt at speed. Sam's body jack-knifed as she dove and he could see as he glanced behind that she was following where he led.

When he looked ahead again, he couldn't see Jamie at all.

A turquoise and black fish suddenly bumped against his cheek, its touch strangely disturbing in the shadowy waters near the dock. The water was disturbed also, churned up by the waves crashing against the water break. Sand and silt swirled upward from the murky bottom, until only his arm was visible as he reached through the water.

He felt a sudden desire to rise to the surface, to spit the snorkel from his mouth and cry out Jamie's name. If anything happened to the child . . . Ice tapped Nate's heart.

He was breathing now in uneven gasps, and with each intake of air, water swirled down his snorkel from the waves slapping the dock. The water had risen above the air intake valve and flowed into his mouth, but he had no time to surface. He blew out the salty liquid as best he could and carried on.

A gnarled, barnacle-encrusted piling suddenly reared before him. To the left of the piling, on the side facing the open water, he could see Jamie's feet. They were thrashing wildly, as though struggling to propel the child to the surface.

Correcting his direction, Nate swam with every ounce of energy he had, racing through the water as single-mindedly as a shark. It was even darker beneath the pier, the gloom exacerbated by swirling sand and seaweed.

Suddenly, frighteningly, the boy's feet stopped moving.

Mustering a strength he didn't know he possessed, Nate pressed harder, reaching for Jamie with a desperation born of fear.

The child was too low, his snorkel topped by two feet of water. Taking a deep breath, Nate dove downward, trying not to think of the seconds ticking off, or of lungs filled with water, or the paleness of the child's skin. Something was anchoring Jamie, and when Nate reached his limp body, he could see what it was.

An arc of fish food floated from the boy's right hand, where it lay locked in the gap between two splintering logs. From the school of sunfish visible between the logs, it was obvious the boy had been reaching for them, entranced as a prospector by their golden colour.

The fish darted around Jamie's fingers, sneaking in like thieves to feed off the food still clinging to his hand.

Nate's lungs threatened to burst. Taking hold of the boy's wrist, he tried to pry the hand back out through the gap. How Jamie had ever got it in was impossible to imagine, for Nate couldn't budge it now. It must have swollen in Jamie's attempts to get free.

Despair crashed at Nate's heart. He had to shift the wood. Even half an inch might do.

Suddenly Sam appeared beside him, and despite the sand swirling between them, he could see the fear in her eyes. But beyond the fear lay trust.

He couldn't let her down, couldn't let the child down, either. He'd been unable to save Jenny and the baby. He couldn't let death claim Jamie too.

He swiftly motioned to Sam to take hold of Jamie's hand, then releasing his own grip on the child, he grasped the piling instead. Swimming close, he wrapped his legs around it in an attempt to gain leverage. Then holding firm to the two upright logs, he pulled with all his might.

At first there was no movement; then, signalled by a mist of sand floating up from the ocean floor, the piling on his right moved an infinitesimal amount. Enough for Sam to lift Jamie's hand up and out.

With lungs ready to explode, Nate grabbed Jamie around his waist and sped to the surface. Swimming like a sea nymph, Sam sped along beside him, surfacing when he did and gulping in some air.

With oxygen in his own lungs, Nate placed his lips over Jamie's mouth. Breathing in, then out, he fought for the life of the child resting limply in his mother's outstretched arms.

The seconds passed like hours, but the colour of Jamie's skin remained a pale white. Nate fought back his fear and persevered, not daring to look at Sam, not wanting to see the terror again in her eyes. Then, with a suddenness that shocked, the child's eyes fluttered open.

'Jamie!' his mother cried.

The boy spewed up a stream of water and gulped in air.

Sam ripped off her mask and pressed

her head against her son's cheek. Relief replaced fear, and when she looked straight at Nate, gratitude beaconed towards him.

'Mom,' Jamie sobbed, then coughed so hard his body shook.

'Shh, son, don't talk.' Sam cuddled his body closer.

Nate moved closer too, and putting his arm around Sam's waist, slowly swam them both toward the shore.

Sam's legs buckled when they finally got there. Nate tightened his grip on her waist, straining to hold both her and Jamie upright while Sam regained her strength. Finally, slowly, she was able to move, and kicking off their flippers, they all made their way out of the sea.

Jamie's face regained its colour as oxygen surged through him, and he wiggled in his mother's arms.

'Give him to me,' Nate said, letting go of Sam and holding out his arms for her son.

Sam's eyes widened, but after a

moment's hesitation, she handed Nate her child.

'Are you ready to stand, Jamie?' Nate asked, keeping his voice matter-of-fact.

'Yes,' the boy replied.

'Right.' Nate sank to his knees and eased Jamie out of his arms and down onto the ground beside him. 'Take your time,' he cautioned, as the boy tried to rise.

'We should get a blanket,' Sam said, squatting on the sand also, looking as though she were going to bundle her son back into her arms.

'I don't need a blanket,' Jamie protested, but he shivered as he spoke, and his skin erupted in hundreds of goose bumps.

'Take my towel,' Nate offered, reaching behind him to the pile of belongings they'd left on the beach. He tucked the towel around the boy's shoulders, noting with satisfaction that he didn't shrug it off.

'What were you doing going off by yourself?' Sam asked Jamie, her voice sharp with anxiety now her child was safe.

'Feeding the fish.' Jamie's eyes grew troubled. 'There was one little one that wasn't getting any of the food. And then a great big one came and chased it away. So I swam after it.' He hung his head. 'I didn't think it would go so far.'

'You've got to stay with other people when you swim, buddy,' Nate said gently. 'But I saw the fish you were talking about. He was pretty cool. And he was eating like a pig from all the food you gave him.' He patted Jamie's shoulder. 'Just make sure you call your mom or me next time, and we'll go with you.'

'Really?' the boy asked, his eyes lighting up.

'Really,' Nate assured him.

With a contented sigh, Jamie snuggled closer to his mother. Sam gazed at Nate over her son's head, her eyes again beaming her thanks.

A warmth stole over Nate that he tried to pretend had nothing to do with the pair beside him. But pretence was impossible. He'd felt something when he held the boy in his arms, and something even greater when he held the boy's mother.

It was a feeling he'd sworn never to experience again.

'I better take these back,' he said gruffly. He stood and stacked their flippers and snorkels together, then strode down the beach away from Sam, not looking at her now, not daring.

★　★　★

Nate picked up the beer the bartender handed him and rested the cool bottle against his forehead. Things were spiralling out of control. He didn't like it.

Problem was Sam Feldon was too damned attractive.

It was impossible to be around her and not notice how her hair had a tendency to curl around her ears, and how her lower lip jutted out when she was cross or confused. It made him want to kiss her pout away.

He should have realized the danger of her attraction while still in Seattle, before inviting her on this cruise and getting entangled in her life.

Nate gulped a mouthful of beer and dug his toes into the sand. The grass roof of the beach bar kept his face in the shade, but the sun still beat hot on his lower legs.

He had to do something about his reaction to Sam, about the lust clouding his brain whenever she was near. He'd hoped the beer's icy coolness would clarify his mind, but the image of Sam's face as she held her boy in her arms set off an ache he couldn't ignore.

If she wasn't so damned vulnerable, and at the same time so damned competent, he wouldn't be tipping ass-over-backwards trying to figure her out, wouldn't have her on his mind at all.

Maybe that was the answer. Rid her from his mind.

'Damn,' he swore softly, dropping his head into his hands.

The broad-shouldered bartender slowly wiped out a glass with a clean rag, then picked up a bottle of rum. 'Get this down *ya, mon*,' he said, his black eyes sympathetic as he poured Nate a shot. 'If it's woman trouble *ya* got, you're *gonna* need it.'

Nate nodded his thanks and poured the rum down his throat. It burned, but the burning felt good, like a back fire hoping to squelch a prairie blaze.

He'd have to forget Sam Feldon if he was going to do the job he'd come for, would have to place her back behind her anonymous oak desk and get her the hell out of his mind.

The few women he'd known since Jenny had died had been easy to forget. A little dinner, some conversation, and what happened after that didn't matter much to either party. Footloose and fancy free was how he liked it. How he wanted to live. It was the only way he could live.

But Sam was different, and perhaps she was as disconcerted as he by the attraction between them. For she was attracted to him. He could see it in her eyes. The only difference was, she didn't want what he wanted. She didn't want a mate who would make no demands, a mate she didn't love. She'd no doubt be as happy as he to nip this attraction in the bud.

Perhaps the only way was to give in to their desires. Perhaps then they could purge this need from their systems, could move on to other people to whom they were more suited.

Nate swallowed another mouthful and the rum burned a little less. Sam knew how he felt about love and marriage, for he'd made his feelings on the subject perfectly clear. If they were attracted to one another, if they acted on those feelings, they'd be doing it with their eyes wide open.

Perhaps making love would douse the

fire raging between them, and after they were done, they could go their separate ways.

He could stop worrying about whether or not she'd be hurt. Whether he'd be hurt also. Keep it casual, unimportant — then move on to marry someone who didn't twist his insides into knots.

'I was beginning to get worried.'

Nate whirled to find Sam standing beside him. He felt slightly dizzy from the speed of the motion. 'What about?' he asked.

'You didn't come back.'

'I thought I'd get us all a drink.'

Sam glanced at the empty rum glass in his right hand and the beer bottle in his left.

'Thought I'd have one myself first,' he muttered, furious at himself for apologizing. He shouldn't care what she thought, shouldn't allow himself to care. He tapped the glass on the bar and motioned to the bartender for a refill.

'Where's Jamie?' he asked, a new

drink in his hand.

'Back on the bus,' she replied coolly.

This wasn't going as planned. He was supposed to be seducing her not fighting with her over nothing. Only, his head had begun to pound and his skin felt too tight for his body.

'By himself?' he asked.

'Grams and Charlie are with him.' Sam smiled faintly. 'I found them walking along the beach with their shoes off. Grams looked about sixteen.'

'She's having a good time.' He returned Sam's smile. It was easier now, talking about someone else.

'I hope so.' Sam's eyes clouded. 'I hope she's not building up this Charlie fellow into something he's not.'

'Don't worry about Ruby. She knows what she's doing.'

'I'm not sure anybody ever knows.'

'Not every man is out to break a woman's heart.'

'No?'

'No,' he said firmly, though his own heart pounded.

'Then why are you avoiding me?'

'I'm not.'

'You are!'

'Why would I do that?' He had been right. She *was* attracted to him as he was to her.

'You know why.' Her eyes turned the deepest blue he'd ever encountered.

'I don't know anything.' He only knew he wanted to kiss this woman, and when he finished doing that would want to start all over again.

'Glad to hear you finally admit it,' Sam murmured.

'Mistake number one,' Nate joked, slowly leaning towards her.

'You're way past number one.' Her expression grew serious. 'I wanted to thank you,' she whispered.

'For what?' He hadn't noticed before the tiny mole on her left cheek. He noticed it now. Concentrating on it was the only thing stopping him from capturing her lips with his.

'You saved my son.'

'You did that as much as me.' He

could smell her now, a scent as tangy as wildflowers growing by the sea.

'I didn't.' Her expression grew bleak. 'I didn't even notice he was gone.'

'Kids are as slippery as fish. You've got to keep them netted up to keep them safe.'

She chewed her bottom lip.

His pulse raced at the gesture.

'One minute he was beside me, and the next — ' Her lips shook.

'Forget it.' He reached for her, placed two fingers across her mouth to stop her from talking. Beneath his fingers, her lips were soft and full, seemed to pulse with a beat that ate into his soul. 'He's fine now,' he assured her.

'Thanks to you,' Sam whispered.

Her words vibrated against his fingers. Then she took his hand in hers and pulled it away. Leaning forward, she moved to kiss him on the cheek.

A quick twist of his head and the cheek became his mouth. Once alighted there, she made no move to leave. Softly, slowly, as sea grass waving in a breeze, his mouth roved over hers.

She seemed, at first, too stunned to kiss him back, then with a suddenness that stole his breath, her lips parted to allow him access. Slowly, so as not to frighten, so as to fully savour the delights within, he explored the edge of her lips. Then his tongue flickered inside, meeting her tongue in an explosion of desire.

His breath disappeared, and along with it all thought, leaving only the sweet sensation that at last he'd come home.

She pulled away.

'Another kiss and we'll call it even,' he suggested in a low murmur.

'Another kiss and we'll be way past even.'

Her eyes were wide and dark, and she probed his face intently.

'Best to build up credit,' he said, seeking her mouth again.

# 11

'Things have changed,' Ruby accused, following Sam into her cabin.

Sam dumped her beach bag beside her bed and wished her grandmother had gone with Nate and Jamie to play video games in the ship's activity room. She wanted to be alone, to fling herself on her bed and think about the kisses she and Nate had shared.

'Nothing's changed,' she protested, although she knew in her heart everything had. It wasn't just the kiss, or the fact that Nate had saved her son. It was more to do with the realization that no matter how wrong Nate was for her, she couldn't stop needing him ... wanting him ... loving him.

'Nothing's changed,' she said again, in a whisper this time, for one thing hadn't changed. No matter how much she loved Nate, she still couldn't have him.

'Jamie told me what happened,' her grandmother said. She sank into Sam's armchair and crossed her arms over her stomach.

Not everything, Sam thought, her face flaming hot. Jamie didn't know about the kiss or how her lips and tongue still tingled from locking with Nate's.

'Nate was wonderful,' Sam said, because she had to say something. Her grandmother had always been able to sense when things were wrong. No use expecting anything different now.

'He saved Jamie's life,' her grandmother reminded her.

'Yes,' Sam said hoarsely. She would never forget her son's near brush with death.

'He's a good man,' Ruby went on.

'Yes,' Sam said again.

'He cares about you.'

'He cares about all his employees.'

'Not like this.'

'Exactly like this!'

'This is different,' Ruby said decisively, 'and you know it. You and Jamie mean something to him. You've only got to look at his face when he looks at you to see that!'

She had seen it, Sam realized, with a lurch of her heart. Unless what she'd seen had been simply lust. God knows, it had been so long since she'd fallen for a man, she probably couldn't tell the difference.

'We kissed,' she admitted softly, saying the one thing she'd vowed never to reveal.

Ruby's eyes lit up, and she leaned forward in her chair.

'That's all really,' Sam added.

'But you wanted more?'

'No . . . yes . . . I don't know.'

'You'd better make up your mind, girl, or you'll lose him.'

'If he's that easily lost, he's not worth having!'

'Do you love him?'

Those were the words she'd only whispered in her head, had been afraid to even think, let alone speak aloud.

'Yes,' she admitted hoarsely.

'I can't hear you.'

'Yes,' she said again, more decisively this time. Then staring bemusedly into her grandmother's delighted face, she said it once again, 'Yes!'

'So what are you going to do about it?'

'Do?'

'Yes, do! Time's-a-wasting.'

'What can I do?' Sam asked, frowning.

'Mercy, child, it's a good thing I'm on this voyage too.' Ruby stood and moved to the telephone sitting on a small desk. Picking it up, she shouted orders over her shoulder as she dialled. 'Get yourself out of those beach things and into the shower. I'll make all the arrangements.'

★　★　★

Lying naked on her stomach with her face in a hole had not seemed the route

252

to bliss, nor had this pummelling and mauling of her muscles. But it felt good. More than good. Even her embarrassment at discovering the masseuse was a man had filtered away in the suspended time of this dimly lit room.

And the whale softly calling from the hidden ceiling stereo seemed to echo her own cries. For love, for happiness, for the joy she deserved.

'You're in knots,' the masseur chided, probing with oiled knuckles into the muscle below Sam's right shoulder.

'Oomph,' Sam replied, her voice muffled by the table. She didn't want to speak anyway, wanted only to lie still and let the tensions flee her body.

She felt wanton laying there, her only covering a thin cotton sheet, but if she was going to seduce Nate as her grandmother suggested, she had to get used to wanton, had to remember how it felt to make love.

'And here,' the masseur added, caressing the tendons around her neck with fingers smelling faintly of rose oil. Then he turned his attentions to her back, pulling the sheet lower and working down her spine in a methodical sweep.

'Better?' he asked at last, drawing the sheet up.

Sam slowly lifted her head. 'Yes,' she said, meaning it, feeling as smooth and supple as she had in her teens, and despite the aura of calm that had silenced her soul, she could feel the blood coursing through her as though in preparation for making love.

'Fine,' the young man said, a smile emerging on his handsomely chiselled face. 'I'll leave you to get into your robe.' He blew out the scented candle. 'Take your time. There's no hurry.'

She couldn't have hurried if she'd wanted to, for despite the tingling of her skin, she felt serenely legless, as content as the mother of a newborn babe.

Clutching her sheet around her, she rolled off the table and slowly pulled on her robe. Then she opened the door and made her way back down the hall to the waiting room.

She had tried to explain to her grandmother that none of this was necessary, but Ruby had insisted. Had said that for once in her life her granddaughter was going to get the best life had to offer, and that if it took the entire afternoon, Sam was going to the Captain's Ball tonight looking like a million bucks.

'Which is about what it's going to cost you,' Sam had protested.

'Never mind that,' her grandmother had responded gaily. 'I won at blackjack last night — almost two thousand dollars — and if I want to spend it on you, I will!'

At which point she'd booked appointments so fast, Sam's head had spun.

★ ★ ★

'Darling,' Fay purred, lifting one brow and shifting position in one of the waiting room's wicker chairs. 'I didn't expect to see you here.'

'Not my usual haunt,' Sam laughingly agreed. Although it certainly was Fay's. Even as a girl she'd had the money to indulge in beauty shop primping.

'You're so natural-looking,' Fay went on, her praise damning in its faintness, 'so practical.' Her eyes narrowed as she scrutinized Sam's face. 'I didn't think you'd waste your time on this sort of nonsense.'

Sam shrugged, remembering now that the thing that had always irritated her the most about Fay was her ability to go straight to the nub of a person's vulnerabilities and expose them wide for all the world to see.

'Is it a special occasion tonight?' Fay asked.

Sam shrugged. She didn't want to talk of Nate to others, wanted to keep all thought of him to herself.

'Have you got a date?' Fay probed again.

'No,' Sam denied. It was something

better than a date. When she and Nate had parted on the beach, he had whispered in her ear to save all her dances that evening for him.

'How's your boss doing?' Fay inquired.

Heat hit Sam's cheeks. 'What do you mean?'

'Is he engaged yet?'

'Not yet.' She couldn't think of engagements. It was enough to know she loved him.

'How was his lunch date?'

'She didn't show up.'

'Really?'

'She got delayed.'

'So is he going to the Captain's cocktail party tonight?'

'We both are.'

'I'll see you there then.' Fay flashed Sam a smile and rose as one of the hairdressers beckoned her to another chair.

Sam watched as her classmate chatted to the woman attending her. Fay obviously liked Nate, and was not averse to showing it, would no doubt appear at the party tonight looking as wonderful as always.

Sam swallowed hard. She could look wonderful too.

She squared her shoulders. She wasn't sixteen anymore. Nor was she lacking in confidence. She was here to get the works, and when it was over, she'd look the best she possibly could for a night of romance with the man she loved.

An hour and a half later and she was nowhere near done. Pursuing beauty was as time-consuming as it was expensive, which was probably why she had never before indulged in a spa treatment. But it was pleasurable, Sam decided, sighing contentedly.

A manicurist had applied scarlet polish to her finger and toe nails, matching the colour of the slip dress her grandmother had bought for her at the on-board boutique. Then had come a facial, and now all that remained was her hair.

The seaweed scalp treatment had sounded repugnant when Sam's grandmother had first mentioned it, but Ruby had urged Sam to have it, saying Fay had told her there was nothing like it for rendering hair silky.

Silky, or not, the best part of all, Sam decided, was the sensation of doing nothing, of finally having the time and privacy to think about Nate and her burgeoning feelings for him.

Her friend Cheryl had often scolded Sam for thinking too much about things, insisting all that ruminating was bad for her brain. Her friend believed things had to happen without so much thought, or you ran the risk of doing nothing at all.

Cheryl would be proud of her this time, Sam decided smugly, even if it had been Sam's grandmother who'd pushed her into these spa appointments, and had insisted, too, that Sam tell Nate how she felt.

Something she hadn't yet managed to do.

What she'd experienced on the beach had terrified her beyond reason, and it wasn't just the danger her son had been in. It was kissing Nate as she had, as though he was all she'd want from now until the day she died, and if she couldn't have him, she didn't want anyone else.

She was sure Nate felt the same. She'd been positive of that from the moment his lips touched hers, and it was that certainty that had convinced her to go along with her grandmother's suggestions, to enjoy being in love and to trust in that love.

Not something she'd experienced in a very long time. If she ever had at all! Her feelings for Phil had been nothing to what she now felt for Nate.

'How are you doing?'

Sam jumped at the sudden reappearance of the beauty spa technician. She hadn't seen the girl enter the room or heard her either. This type of girl with her too-short black skirt that had a slit extending clear up to her panty line, and a top that skimmed the area well above her belly button, should enter a room jangling, not silently as a ghost.

Shouldn't eighteen years, at least, be a minimum age requirement? Sam wondered dazedly. This girl, with her spiked hair and violently coloured makeup, looked younger than Sam had ever looked, though she was finding it increasingly difficult to remember anything of life prior to the birth of Jamie.

Her son's arrival had been such a profound event she'd left childhood behind without a backward glance.

'Fine,' Sam said faintly, answering the girl at last, hoping this intrusion into her peace would be short-lived. She didn't want to talk yet, didn't want anything but blissful solitude.

'Great,' the girl replied, the word ending with the sound of bubble gum cracking. 'You've got a few minutes yet.' She moved toward the panel controlling the aria of piped-in flutes. 'A little louder?' she asked, twisting up the volume and flashing Sam another don't-slow-me-down grin before scurrying out the door.

'No,' Sam replied slowly to the already empty room, wincing as the flute hit a particularly high note. That was another thing that had changed since she'd become a mother. After a day engulfed in the sounds of an excited eight-year-old, all she wanted in the way of sound was no sound at all.

Shutting her eyes, Sam tried to recapture the effects of the flute's hypnotic beat. If she could fall asleep again, could lose herself in her own subconscious, then her worries about seeing Nate and admitting to him how she felt might disappear. She might even be able to trust that he would say the words she needed to hear, the words she was sure were in his heart.

Breathing in slowly, she willed her body to relax . . .

'Oh, my God!'

The beautician's horror-struck voice jarred Sam awake.

'What's wrong?' she stammered,

trying to fight her way through the cotton batting encasing her mind. Sam struggled to sit straight, but it took a few seconds to even figure out where she was. And when she did, she realized at once that she didn't want to be there, not if it meant being the object of the beautician's wide-eyed stare.

'What's wrong?' she asked again, sternly this time. She spoke as she would to Jamie when he was upset and unable to explain why.

'Nothing,' the girl said. Her face turned pale. 'I hope.'

Sam peered at the tag pinned to the girl's blouse. 'Tillie,' she read aloud, 'what do you mean?'

The girl was moving at high speed now, all laconic swivelling of hips a thing of the past. She pulled the plastic off Sam's head and began to unwind the seaweed wrap.

'Oh!' she gasped again, and her eyes filled with tears. 'It's not my fault, Miss,' she faltered. 'I told Margie I didn't have time. But she wouldn't listen. She never listens.'

'Time to do what?'

'To shampoo her client,' Tillie wailed. 'I've been telling you!'

'You haven't told me a thing.'

'Margie said to take her client to chair number five. That's not my station,' she said indignantly, 'and I told her Angie wouldn't like it. Angie's our boss,' she explained. 'When she finds out — ' Her lips trembled. ' — she's going to fire me.'

'I still don't know what's happened.'

'I'm telling you. Margie said to wash the woman's hair and settle her under the dryer. She said the woman would make it worth my while.'

'You were bribed?'

'She didn't pay me anything.'

'I don't understand. Did you get shampoo in the woman's eyes, or what?' The beginnings of a headache tugged at Sam's temples.

'This isn't about the woman.'

'Then why are we talking about her?'

'I . . . I wanted to explain why I've

been late getting back to you.'

'It's all right,' Sam said gently. 'I'm not in that much of a hurry. I still need my hair trimmed, but that won't take long.' She glanced at her watch. 'The Captain's cocktail party isn't until eight.'

Tillie's face flushed scarlet, and she pulled off the last of the seaweed wrap.

'What is it?' Sam asked again, as Tillie's red face turned white.

'I didn't mean to,' the girl sobbed.

'Get me a mirror,' Sam ordered. She reached up a hand to touch her hair. It certainly felt the same. Only better. Softer. Possibly even thicker. She breathed a little easier. Whatever it was, she wasn't bald.

Tillie held the mirror up to Sam's face.

She didn't recognize, at first, the image reflected there, and when she did, her breath fled her lungs.

'It's green!' Sam gasped, her mirror eyes widening.

'Not so green,' Tillie whispered, but

her voice lacked conviction.

'Green,' Sam repeated, panting to find air. 'How?'

'I must have left the wrap on too long,' Tillie said miserably. 'And — '

'And what?' Oxygen, at last, crept into Sam's lungs, but it burnt as it went in, unlike any air she'd ever known.

'Something Margie said when I told her she could do her own clients in future as I had a client under a seaweed wrap and she should have been out twenty minutes ago.'

'What did she say?'

'She asked if I'd done a seaweed scalp treatment before.'

'And?'

'I've seen it done,' Tillie said defiantly.

'Here?'

'No.' The girl bit her lip. 'At beautician's school.'

'When did you graduate?' Perhaps if she asked questions, she could keep her mind from reeling.

'Last month,' Tillie said proudly.

'This is my first job.'

'Then why are they letting you do complicated procedures like this?'

'We're short-staffed,' Tillie explained. 'One of the girls is down with the flu and another went on shore leave and didn't come back. They say her boyfriend's disappeared, too, the one who works in the engine room.'

'Tillie,' Sam said warningly, her head spinning from the flow of words.

'Anyway,' the girl continued hastily, 'that's why I had to do you. Angie got called to the Purser's Office, and Margie was doing a streaking job, and you'd just come out from having your nails done, and Margie said to take you down here. When I asked what you were scheduled for and she said a seaweed scalp treatment, I thought I'd just do it — ' The girl's face was a picture of misery. 'I thought they'd be happy. Margie's always complaining I show no initiative.' A tear dripped down her cheek. 'I thought I would show her.'

Tillie's shoulders drooped and she let

the mirror drop.

Which was one thing at least for which she was thankful, Sam decided.

Then the girl took a deep breath and continued on. 'After I got you set up, I went out into the main spa for a minute and was told to finish up Margie's client. I tried to tell Margie I didn't have time but she wouldn't listen. And her client scared me worse. I'd heard red-heads have tempers, but — ' She winced. ' — this woman wasn't very nice.'

'What did Margie tell you?' If Sam heard one more word about redheads and shampoos, she'd wind up shaking Tillie.

'She told me blondes aren't supposed to have seaweed scalp treatments — '

'So why didn't anyone tell me that when I asked for it?'

'We've been so busy,' Tillie wailed again. 'And what with the Captain's cocktail party and New Year's Eve tomorrow, everyone's been getting their hair done today. When you asked for the wrap, the receptionist probably assumed you'd had one before, and I — ' Her bottom lip looked raw from the worrying her teeth was giving it. ' — didn't know any better.'

'Didn't know,' Sam repeated dully.

'It sometimes turns blonde hair green,' Tillie whispered. 'You'd have been better off with the Aloe treatment.'

Was this a sign? Sam wondered. Was loving Nate and having a relationship with him so impossible it was ridiculous even to try? Was it as ridiculous as this sea-green hair hanging around her shoulders?

If she hadn't convinced herself that a man like Nate, who wanted nothing to do with love, could fall for a woman like her, who believed love was the only answer, she'd never have got into this mess in the first place.

If she hadn't listened to her grandmother, whose enthusiasm for matchmaking had always ended disastrously in the past, she wouldn't be sitting here with green hair.

She picked up the mirror and stared again at her reflection, her spirits sinking lower with the second look. She had wanted to look beautiful, had wanted to sweep Nate off his feet and finish what they had begun on the beach. Had wanted to change him, to show him love was something to be cherished, not thrown away before he had even opened the package.

She still wanted that.

Perhaps her emerald hair was a test, not a sign at all! Perhaps despite how dreadful she looked, she had to go to Nate and give them both the opportunity to explore their feelings.

'Where are the scissors?' she demanded.

'Scissors?' Tillie asked, eyeing Sam as though deciding it might be prudent to remove all sharp instruments from her vicinity.

'We're going to cut it off,' Sam said.

'Maybe we could dye over it.' Tillie's voice was as dubious as the expression in her eyes.

'What colour would cover this green?'

'Black,' Tillie replied, her eyes narrowing.

Sam gulped back the hysteria rising in her throat. With pale skin and black hair, she'd look like a witch.

'How long would it take?' she managed to ask calmly.

'An hour, hour and a half — '

Hope fled Sam's body as fast as it had entered, and the desire grew stronger to retreat to her room and never emerge again.

'That's too long,' she said. Then she straightened her shoulders. 'Get Margic,' she ordered.

Tillie scuttled from the room, glancing back at the door as though hoping against hope the nightmare hair would disappear.

Sam rose from her chair and began to pace, averting her eyes from all shiny surfaces, not wanting to see again the extent of the disaster. The flutes still warbled, but now they weren't soothing. At the sound of the door opening, she whirled around.

'What seems to be the — '

Hysteria threatened again at the look of shock on Margie's face.

'What have you done?' the older beautician roared, turning on Tillie.

'Never mind what,' Sam interjected. 'How are we going to fix it?'

'Fix it?' the woman sputtered, her plump features quivering.

'Yes, fix it,' Sam said firmly, glancing again at her watch. 'The Captain's cocktail party begins in an hour.'

'I'm sorry, Madam but — '

'But what?' Sam asked softly.

'I'm sure you're upset — ' Margie took a step backward and bumped into Tillie. ' — but we can't fix this in an hour.' She smoothed her hands over her smock as if that action might smooth Sam's ruffled feelings. 'The Salon will be happy to refund Madam's money — '

'I don't want a refund.'

Margie shot Tillie a venomous glance. ' — and I can assure you Miss

Park will be dismissed immediately.'

'That's not what I want, either.'

'But she — '

'She explained the risks,' Sam lied, keeping her gaze steady and sure. 'I chose to ignore them.' Her skin felt tight. 'But I can't go to the Captain's party looking like this.'

'A dye job takes time — '

'I know. Tillie told me.'

'And even if we were to do it, I doubt we could cover that green effectively with anything but black.'

'Then we'll have to cut it off.'

'Cut it off?' Margie gasped.

'Short,' Sam said, 'with tapered sides.' She looked in the mirror and swallowed hard. 'Make that punk,' she instructed, before she could change her mind. 'Make it look as though this were done on purpose.'

'But Madam — '

'Kids all over the country are dying their hair green. Why not me?'

'You're hardly a — '

'We're wasting time.' Sam pushed

past her and walked out of the room. To her relief, the two beauticians followed.

Within minutes, Sam's head was under a tap and Tillie was shampooing so hard it was as though she were attempting to take the colour out by force. Then she bundled Sam into a chair behind a plastic palm.

So nobody else would see her, Sam thought, with a sigh. In case the sight of her hair was so appalling it scared away prospective clients. With a frown, she watched Margie gather up her scissors and approach her chair.

'I want Tillie to cut it,' Sam said firmly.

'But — '

With a shake of her head, Sam cut the woman's protests short.

'Are you sure?' Tillie asked, looking very young and vulnerable.

'Totally,' Sam replied.

Taking the scissors from Margie's hand, the girl ran a comb through Sam's hair and cut off a long curl. It hung glistening from Tillie's fingers in the salon's bright light then floated to the floor like the feather from a peacock.

Sam's gut curled as inch after inch of hair fluttered to the floor, piling in peaks like waves in the ocean.

'A bit shorter?' Tillie asked, still snipping furiously.

It was already shorter than it had been since Sam was six, and the back of her neck felt cold where her hair had been shorn. It speared up on top like a field of un-mown grass, but despite its strangeness, something about the cut appealed to her, seemed fresh in a funky way.

'Short enough,' she finally said, tilting her head to the left. 'Now, what about some of those little hair slides?'

'These?' Tillie asked, pulling forward a clip board of coloured glass angels on sticks.

'Exactly!'

Tillie pinned a couple onto her hair.

Sam grinned at her reflection. The Lord only knew how Nate would react at the sight of her, but despite looking as though she were as young as Tillie, it was a rush trying something new. It had been a long time since she had dared.

It must be the cruise which was romantic, exotic, ripe with possibilities. She had changed. Was grasping for things she hadn't reached for before. Was prepared to trust her heart now and allow her love for Nate to grow.

'Done!' Tillie exclaimed. She pulled off the plastic cape from around Sam's shoulders.

'Right.' Sam flashed the girl a smile. Red angels twinkled from various spots on her head.

'You look wonderful!' Tillie enthused.

'It's not what I had in mind when I made the appointment — ' She grinned up at Tillie. ' — but I like it.'

# 12

Once back in her own cabin, she wasn't as sure.

'What do you think?' Sam asked her grandmother. The top of her head seemed even greener now than it had in the salon, and wearing the red slip dress, she looked like a Christmas elf.

'It's as good a time as any to find out if Nate has a sense of humour,' Ruby replied dryly.

Sam groaned.

'I'm betting he has,' her grandmother added.

'I'm not sure it even matters,' Sam said dubiously, attempting to tuck a lock of hair behind her ear.

'You've got it bad,' Ruby said sympathetically.

'I'm not even sure how it happened,' Sam said, with a sigh. 'I only know that I love him.' She glanced fiercely at her grandmother. 'But you're not to tell him I told you so.'

'I wouldn't dream of it.'

Sam turned back to the mirror. 'I'll tell him myself.' She'd visualized how she would do it, and how Nate would look when he told her he loved her too.

'Are you sure about how you feel?' Ruby asked gently.

'I've never been more certain of anything in my life.'

'And Nate?'

'I don't know.' But she remembered his warmth when he had pulled her to him, and how his eyes had grown dark.

'Right, then,' her grandmother said, rising from her chair. 'Are you ready?'

'You go up first. Charlie will be waiting.'

Anticipation lit her grandmother's face.

Sam smiled. She wasn't the only one to have fallen in love on this voyage. 'I want to say good night to Jamie first.'

'I don't know how you've convinced him it's time to go to bed.'

'I haven't,' Sam replied. 'The kids' club is putting on their own party for the kids. A swim, then a movie, then games in the arcade room.'

'Tell Jamie I'll collect him at eleven o'clock.' Her grandmother patted her hair smooth and moved toward the door.

'Won't Charlie mind?'

'Charlie said he'd help babysit.' Ruby grinned. 'He's promised to teach Jamie some card tricks.'

'Sounds like the two of you are getting close.'

'We are,' Ruby admitted, 'but if he's going to be involved in my life, he's going to have to be involved in Jamie's life also. In your life, too.'

'I don't want you worrying about Jamie and me, Grams. If this thing — '

'Thing?' Ruby's eyes twinkled.

'Romance, then.'

'You've got to learn to say the word,' her grandmother teased, 'if you're going to have one yourself.'

'You're right.' Sam straightened her

shoulders. 'I'll force myself.'

'Good girl,' Ruby said, and with a swift caress of Sam's cheek, she was out the door.

★  ★  ★

If Sam had been in doubt as to in which ballroom the Captain's cocktail party was being held, the music wafting down the deck would have told her.

Music played for romance, she decided contentedly. Then with a shiver, she leaned against the railing and listened. Despite the calm air and the day's heat still cloaking the night, she suddenly felt cold.

Must be nerves, she told herself sternly. It was one thing to know how she felt, to make a guess as to how Nate felt, but quite another to admit it to him.

A seagull swooped close to where she stood, followed closely by another, their paths elegant and synchronized.

As Nate's and her path could be if

only she had the courage.

She squared her shoulders and moved toward the ballroom. The morning had been so right, and the afternoon had gone so wrong, but despite the colour of her hair, she'd do all in her power to make the evening perfect.

Her dress was gorgeous, and even her hair made her feel something wild and wonderful was about to happen, something fabulous that would match her extraordinary appearance.

And that something would include Nate.

He would take her into his arms and whirl her around the dance floor. Despite their differences of opinion on the nature of marriage, they would look into each other's eyes and find the love they both needed.

Love could change anything Sam told herself firmly, could change anybody. It certainly had her. The old Sam wouldn't have dared to put her love on the line, especially if it meant doing so with a head of emerald hair.

And Nate, she was sure, from what she'd seen in his eyes, had felt love's force, also. Surely feeling as he did now, he would rethink his preposterous notion of marriage without love.

She eagerly pushed the doors open and scanned the room. Where was Nate?

She could see her grandmother and Charlie out on the dance floor, dancing too slow to a quickstep. But their faces were alight with happiness as they gazed at each other, and their movements, though slow, were resonant with awareness, as though their bodies tingled from their closeness and the familiar intimacy of lovers.

A warmth clutched Sam's heart and she fought back her tears. Her grandmother deserved this kind of happiness, had waited too long to get it.

As she had herself.

Well, no more. She would find Nate and tell him just how she felt, would tell him that she loved him.

She edged through the crowd lining

the parquet floor, nodding as people greeted her but not stopping to talk. When a passing waiter offered a fluted glass of champagne, she took it almost absently, searching for Nate over its rim, seeking out the man she loved.

Then to her left she heard laughter, the tinkling tones of a woman echoed by the low chuckle of a man. It was Nate's laughter, as firmly printed on Sam's soul as the shape of his lips, and the way his eyes darkened when he felt something deeply, as they had when he had kissed her.

Turning, she spotted him standing with his back to her, leaning nonchalantly against the bar. His shoulders were broad in the confines of his tux, and his unruly hair waved nearly to his collar.

A smile formed on her lips. She took a step forward.

Then she saw the hand.

A woman's hand. It stole from in front of Nate and brushed his hair back from his face.

Sam's smile died.

The disembodied hand reached forward once again, and Sam's throat constricted, blocking all breath. This time the woman's fingers draped the back of his neck, lingering at the edge of his hair, rings sparkling in the light of the chandeliers.

Sam's vision blurred, but even through that, she could see Nate did nothing to prevent the assault on his space.

The warmth fled her body, leaving nothing behind but an icy emptiness.

'There you are!' Ruby exclaimed, from somewhere to Sam's right.

Slowly, stiffly, Sam turned to face her.

Her grandmother's face was wreathed in smiles and her cheeks glowed pink as she moved towards Sam, Charlie in tow.

'Where's Nate?' Ruby asked.

'Don't know,' Sam mumbled.

Ruby halted a passing waiter and plucked champagne from his tray. She passed the fresh glass to Sam then reached for two more for herself and Charlie.

'We wanted you both here when we told you,' Ruby said. She took hold of Charlie's hand, her cheeks flushing darker.

'Told me what?' Sam asked, feeling dead inside. From the corner of her eye she could see Nate still, could see the woman's arm wrapped sinuously around his neck.

'We're getting married,' Ruby replied, raising her left hand and wiggling her fingers. A hefty diamond sparkled from her ring finger. 'Charlie went overboard, of course,' she chided her fiance affectionately. 'I told him I didn't need a diamond, didn't even want a diamond — '

'And I told her, nothing but the best for my girl.' Charlie pulled Sam's grandmother to him and kissed her full on the lips.

For a moment, Sam thought Ruby was going to sink to the floor, but after melting against Charlie for one long moment, she broke off the kiss.

'So we're celebrating!' Ruby went on. 'We'll pay our respects to the Captain then we'll all have dinner together. Just the four of us; Charlie and me, and you and Nate.'

'I'm sorry, Grams — '

'There he is,' Ruby interrupted. 'Yoohoo, Nate!'

Sam twisted around, wanting only to disappear, but equally unable to bear looking away. Nate twisted too and his gaze met hers.

His eyes were dark and hard and his lips were tight. And curled around his arm now was the woman's hand. Then she stepped out from behind him and Sam thought she might faint.

Fay's newly coiffed hair glistened as she leaned against Nate and whispered something into his ear. Then she threw back her head and laughed.

Laughing at her, Sam decided sickly. As Nate was no doubt laughing also.

Her skin prickled. Compared to Fay, she looked about as appealing as a fried green tomato. She couldn't stay here another instant and watch the man she loved fall in love with another woman.

For the way Fay looked at Nate, the way she moved and held him, falling in love was obviously what had happened.

Sam mumbled an apology and whirled away. She fled out the door, not stopping for breath until she'd put a half deck's length between them. Even then she was loath to halt, but she couldn't go further, had no strength to carry on.

She staggered to the railing and leaned against it for support, the shadowy bulk of a lifeboat towering above her on her left. If she could have got it down and out to sea, she would have done so in an instant. She wanted only to put distance between herself and her pain.

For all she felt now was pain. It had swept like a tide into the warmth of her love, and was now seeping wetly into every corner or her being.

She'd been wrong about Nate, had been wrong, too, about how he felt. He didn't love her at all, probably saw her as nothing more than a burden and a nuisance. He'd stated what he wanted from the very beginning and what he wanted was a woman like Fay.

A woman who was perfect for him, who wanted nothing more than what he wanted, too, who didn't need love or commitment to make her life complete.

With Fay's striking good looks, and her dead husband's money, she'd be the perfect wife for Nate. Even the speed with which he'd want to marry would appeal to her impulsive nature, and if the marriage was a failure, she'd simply chalk it up to a fun time had by all.

Sam's fingers clenched the railing, but she found its smooth surface had lost the power to soothe. The gull she'd seen earlier hung in a current beside her, its mate now nowhere to be seen. One more thing about which she'd been wrong. Assuming partnership where it wasn't, expecting love where it couldn't flourish.

With a muted cry, she struck the railing with her hand.

'What the devil are you doing?' Nate growled from behind. 'Looking to be keelhauled for destruction of private property?'

Sam whirled around, found herself face to face with the man she loved. Couldn't love, she amended hastily.

'You've been crying,' he said more softly.

Sam scrubbed at her eyes, pushing away the moisture accumulating there.

'Why?' he demanded.

How could he even ask? Sam gripped her lips in an effort to stop them trembling.

'And what in God's name have you done to your hair?'

'I dyed it,' she said defiantly, sudden anger ousting the tears.

'That's not all!'

'And cut it.'

'Why?'

'I wanted a change.'

'You got that!' He reached out as if to touch her.

'I like it,' she added defiantly, ducking from beneath his hand.

'Who wouldn't?'

'You obviously don't.'

This time he did touch her. He caressed her cheek, and the electricity created caused her breath to flee.

'I do like it,' he murmured, tilting her chin upward.

His eyes were shadowed from the moonlight by the boat beside them, but his fingers tightened on her chin and she could feel his intensity through them.

'Rather green,' she countered softly.

'Seasonal,' he replied, chuckling.

'Are you saying I look like a Christmas tree?'

He laughed out loud this time. Then his laughter died. 'Is that why you ran away from the party?'

'You know why I ran.'

'I looked up and the first and last I saw of you was the back of your head disappearing through the door.'

'You were too busy to notice anything else.'

'That's not true.'

She lifted one brow, not trusting herself to speak.

'I was waiting for you.' He slipped his arm around her waist.

'I saw Fay waiting with you.'

His eyes grew blacker. 'I don't want to talk about Fay.'

'What then?'

'Nothing.' He brushed his fingers over her cheek. 'We talk too much.'

What he said was true. They talked and they talked, but they didn't say what was in their hearts. Maybe the time for talk was past.

'I've been waiting all day to do this,' he murmured, leaning forward.

Any vestige of protest died the moment his lips brushed hers. They barely touched at first, were more a promise than a kiss, but the anticipation filling her body created heat from ice.

Then his lips hardened, and she

could smell as well as taste him, the cool scent of his cologne, the warm touch of champagne, the welcome of the air travelling in and out through his lips.

A physical need swept over her, casting away her doubts. She wanted only to be held in the circle of Nate's arms, and keep on kissing him until her lips could kiss no more. Even then, she doubted it would be enough, doubted her desire would ever be sated.

'It's time we stopped talking,' he said again. 'You know how I feel.'

She thought she had known then had felt something different. Had what she'd seen been wrong, not really the way it was, not really the evidence she'd been afraid of finding that he still intended to follow his plan?

'And I know how you feel,' he added, in a whisper.

How could he not know? She was pressed against him so wantonly there was no room for error. She wanted him so badly it felt like a sickness, only something this wonderful could never be likened to flu.

With a moan, she pressed closer. 'Stop talking,' she commanded. 'Kiss me instead.'

With an answering groan, he did as she directed. Then he swept her into his arms and carried her to his cabin.

They must have passed people along the way dressed in tuxedos and long gowns, but all Sam could see was the silky blackness of Nate's jacket and the way his chin rode high and firm above her green head.

His cabin when they reached it was ready and inviting. The steward had pulled down the blankets and laid a chocolate on each pillow.

'For later,' Nate said, sweeping them away.

He laid her on the bed gently, and without releasing her lay there too. She wasn't sure how they undressed, only knew the frenzy to do so was too primal to refuse.

First shoes, then outer clothing, then

her slip and nylons, until at last she lay clad in her underwear only, as Nate was in his, their lips locked together as though never intending to release.

The moon shone through the cabin window, casting them both in a mixture of light and shadow. They moved slower now, as though suddenly aware that this moment was to be treasured, to be measured out in seconds, not gone through in haste.

Nate ran his hand down Sam's spine, his touch feathery light though his body was hard. 'Sam, I — '

'Shush, don't say a word.'

'But I need to tell you — '

'Tell me like this.'

She pulled him to her, enticing him, encouraging. She had never wanted in this way, had not known what it was to want like this. Making love with Phil had been a swift exchange of bodily fluids, not this roller coaster ride to the dizzying heights of passion.

'Samantha,' Nate whispered, when finally they lay still.

Thrilled by the sound of her name on his lips, Sam pressed her body closer and continued her way to heaven.

# 13

Sam struggled to open her eyes, but the warmth of Nate's bed engulfed her, and the delicious unboned sensation in her limbs made it impossible to exchange the magic of the night before for the promise of the day to come.

She stretched out one arm, searching for the solid strength of Nate's back, or the washboard flatness of his belly. She'd lain in his arms all night, rousing from her slumbers only to drown in their mutual passion, and she wanted him now as she had the night before, couldn't believe the need he still awakened.

'Mom.'

Her son's youthful treble pierced the fog cloaking Sam's brain, and she reacted in the way she'd done since he was born. She yanked down her covers and swung her feet to the floor.

Cool, conditioned air wafted her toes. She laid one foot over the other for warmth and clung to sleep's tail with the tenacity of a mother.

'Mom,' Jamie said again, only louder this time, and his voice was accompanied now by a knock.

He was knocking on the wrong door. Sam cleared the last vestiges of sleep from her eyes. Of course he was. She wasn't in her own room. She was in Nate's room — she spread her fingers over the soft mattress — in Nate's bed.

And her son was across the hall knocking on her bedroom door, looking for her.

As her grandmother must be too, Sam realized with a groan.

'Your mother must have gone up to breakfast already,' Ruby said, her voice muffled by the closed door between them.

Sam glanced toward the window, was stunned to see through a crack in the curtain, the sun already climbing in the sky.

So she had slept, had at some point in the wee hours of the morning fallen into the exhausted contented sleep of a woman in the arms of her lover.

Nate. Sam frowned, and glanced to his side of the bed. Where was he?

Another knock. This time her son rapped a tune on her door, then paused dramatically as if expecting the final bar to be rapped out by her.

She couldn't open Nate's door and face her son's astonished expression. Not now. Not yet. She and Nate had made love, had shown their love to each other, but she wanted to keep it between them for now. It was too new to share.

Even with her family.

Especially with them.

It had been tough enough already for Jamie, longing for a father who had never come back. She couldn't let him see Nate in a father's light. Not until she herself knew how things stood between them. She was sure of her own feelings, but they hadn't yet talked, hadn't come to grips with this new twist to their relationship.

Until they'd done that, she wanted no one to know what she now knew, that after last night her whole life had changed.

Where was Nate?

Suddenly she spotted the note propped against Nate's bedside clock.

Samantha,
I'll be back shortly.
We have to talk.
Nate

Sam pulled her sunglasses from her pocket and slipped them onto her face. Then she pushed open the wooden doors to the Lido deck and swiftly scanned the crowd. No sign of Nate. He was probably at the cappuccino bar ordering them both coffee. She carefully edged past the morning sunbathers and rounded the hot tub. Not there either.

Biting her lip in frustration, Sam

stared toward the shore. St. Thomas harbour was spectacular from where she stood, stretching out before her in a glistening turquoise strip between ship and land, while behind the white-washed town, green hills lushly rose.

They'd be here a full day, would leave sometime after midnight. After New Year's Eve, Sam suddenly realized. The hairs on her arms rose. After New Year's Eve, if Nate wasn't married, his inheritance would go elsewhere.

To an historical society, she remembered.

'Sam!'

She spun around, saw Fay's silk skirt swishing as the other woman approached, but she couldn't see her face, not shaded as it was by a large-brimmed hat.

'Hello, Fay,' Sam replied, fighting back the image of the evening before, of Fay's hands on Nate with the familiarity of a girlfriend, implying an intimacy she now knew didn't exist.

Her ex-classmate had always been

over-the-top friendly with the boys. Obviously things hadn't changed now the boys had become men.

'Wow!' Fay exclaimed. 'I saw your hair last night, but couldn't quite believe it!'

Sam's hand involuntarily rose to her head. She'd forgotten about her hair. Nate had seen to that. But in the bright light of day, its greenness must rival the trees on the distant hills.

'I was in the mood for something drastic,' she replied with a shrug.

'You certainly achieved that!' Then Fay's eyes narrowed and she studied Sam's face. 'What's up?' she suddenly asked.

People said falling in love indelibly wrought changes in a person, gave them a glow and colour nothing else could. Given the way Fay was staring, perhaps it was true.

'Nothing's up,' Sam lied. Nothing except that she'd fallen in love. Had learned to trust again as well. And it was the trust that made the difference, made the love twice as sweet.

'Something's different,' Fay insisted.

This was the other thing she should have remembered about her former classmate: how Fay had a sixth sense when it came to relationships, and a way of extricating information from the object of her attention.

'Nothing,' Sam lied again, averting her head to shield her eyes.

'You've found a man?' her classmate guessed. 'Who is he?'

Sam shrugged, didn't speak.

'Anyone I know?'

Anyone watching them last night would have said Fay knew him well, but the memory of Nate's lips on her own enabled Sam to smile.

'It is a man,' Fay accused triumphantly.

And the memory, too, of his body pressing against hers; hot, firm and exceedingly male.

'I've met someone too,' Fay added smugly.

'That's nice,' Sam murmured.

'Someone you know,' Fay added.

'I don't know anyone.'

'Nate,' Fay went on, in a satisfied tone.

Sam's heart bumped to a stop.

Fay held up her left hand and her eyes sparkled brighter than the diamond crushing her finger. 'We're engaged,' she burbled on. 'It happened last night at the Captain's cocktail party.' Her laughter tinkled out. 'I know what you're going to say — '

It was impossible to breathe, let alone to talk. Sam's mind had shut down completely. All she could do was feel and the feelings were so terrible she wanted to die.

' — that I've already been married twice and should be running scared.' Fay paused dramatically. 'But Nate's different.'

Nate *was* different, although in a way Fay would never appreciate.

'I could fall in love with him,' her classmate went on.

'If you're engaged,' Sam croaked out,

'why aren't you in love already?'

'Maybe I am.' She smiled slowly. 'When he kissed me . . . '

He had kissed her? How could he have kissed Fay then gone on to kiss her? To make love to her? The pain in Sam's chest drove through to her soul.

' . . . it felt nice,' Fay finished.

Nice no more described Nate's kisses than warm described the blistering Caribbean sun. Nate's kisses were thrilling. Sam closed her eyes, tried to hide the pain shooting through her like lightning sears the sky.

'I know it's a crazy,' Fay went on, 'but I like a man who's a little crazy, a little impulsive.'

Was that what she herself meant to Nate, a bit of impulsiveness he'd regretted as soon as the deed was done? Was that why he'd disappeared before she had even woken?

'We're getting married tonight,' Fay continued on. 'We've booked the Justice of the Peace on St. Thomas.'

Married.

Nausea rolled through Sam's belly.

Tonight.

The last night of the year. Nate would get what he wanted, his millions and a wife.

But he wouldn't get her.

He'd already had her, she realized sickly.

Which was probably all he wanted.

While she'd been fooling herself with dreams of family and white picket fences.

'I want you to be there,' Fay added, unclasping her purse and scribbling down an address on a piece of paper. 'You can give me away,' she suggested, with a laugh.

Sam couldn't force her hand forward to touch the paper Fay thrust at her, but the other woman tucked it into Sam's pocket with the speed of a snake.

'You won't feel uncomfortable, will you?' Fay asked. 'Nate being your boss and all.' She tossed her hair back. 'No, of course, you won't. You and he are friends.' She laughed again. 'To think I once thought you and Nate were lovers.'

Nausea rose in Sam's throat. She turned and raced away, shoving past a burly man in polka dot swim trunks.

'Make that a bridesmaid,' Fay trilled after her. 'Eleven p.m., at the Justice of the Peace.'

Sam ran for the elevators and stabbed the down button. She had to get off this ship, had to get away from any possibility of ever seeing Nate again.

Her family too. She could only imagine the pity on Gram's face, the sadness . . . She couldn't bear it. Not now. Not when her heart had been ripped out and flung like garbage to the seagulls flying alongside the ship.

Down the elevator she went, then along the passageway to her right, then down the flight of stairs leading through a narrow door to the ramp connecting the ship with the shuttle boat to shore. The cutter plied through the crowded harbour all day, taking passengers back and forth to the shopping mecca of St. Thomas.

The cutter was already full, but the sailor guarding the ramp took one look at Sam's face and ushered her aboard. Within seconds she was on her way, away from the ship and the man who'd destroyed her dreams.

*   *   *

Everything looked the same, Sam decided dismally, when the cutter returned her later that evening. Even though her heart was broken, nothing had changed.

Only now, instead of sunlight reflecting brightly off the ship's sides, she saw Christmas lights instead twinkling along its railings.

Sam slumped in her seat, her cheek touching the window. The glass was cool, or maybe it was simply that her cheek was hot, a combination of too much sun and boiling emotions.

She'd tried all day to banish Nate

from her mind, to pretend she was a tourist like any other on the island, to stare at the scenery with the fascination it deserved. But it had proved impossible.

No matter what she did or where she went, she'd been reminded of Nate, of his laughter, his enthusiasm, of the tenderness in his eyes. He was buried in her heart now as deeply as Jamie and Grams and no matter how much of a lie she knew last night to be, she couldn't get him out.

The lump expanded in her throat. It would have been better if she'd never come on this trip, if she'd continued to admire Nate from a distance. For to have grown to know him, to love him, to make love to him, and then to find he didn't love her back hurt more than she could bear.

Perhaps if she talked to him the anger and pain she felt inside would erupt and be released. Then she'd be free of this man who could never be hers. Not now. Not engaged to someone else.

The one thing she couldn't do was go to Nate's wedding, couldn't watch him walk down the aisle with Fay at his side.

Better by far for her to simply leave, to gather her family and belongings and fly back to Seattle. Jamie and Grams would do what she asked even if she couldn't tell them why. One look at her face and they'd know not to ask questions.

Her only relief was that Nate's business would be safe, as would Mrs. Mulroy, and Samson, and all the factory employees. They could rest easy knowing their jobs would be secure. She, however, would hand in her notice, couldn't work for Nate, not feeling the way she did.

She stuffed her fist into her mouth to hold back her sobs, realizing at that moment just how much her job meant to her, how hard it would be to leave.

There was no one else near, no one to notice she was crying, but she straightened away from the window and sucked back her pain. She'd survived grief before. She could do it again.

Although losing Phil, the father of her child, had never hurt as much as this, had never laid bare her soul and ripped her life into shreds.

She couldn't rely on her grandmother now either. Not with Ruby engaged to be married. Couldn't even tell Grams what happened for fear the old lady would interfere. Or worse yet, would give up her own happiness to take care of her and Jamie.

Sam couldn't allow that. She would have to find Grams instead and tell her she had to return home, would cite business as the reason, and say Nate needed her back in Seattle. But she'd insist Grams and Jamie stay and finish the voyage out.

No doubt her grandmother would guess a small portion of the truth when Nate showed up in the morning married, but she wouldn't know the whole of it, wouldn't know he and Sam had made love or that she'd given him her heart.

Only to have him throw it back.

Sam shakily stood, then waiting until the shuttle boat sidled up to the ship, moved toward the gangplank bridging the gap between the two vessels.

A young couple disembarked ahead of her, holding hands and laughing. Eager to get to the New Year's Ball, Sam decided gloomily, as she had been looking forward before she discovered the truth.

Her grandmother would be there already, dancing in Charlie's arms. At least someone in her family was happy. At least Grams knew what it was like to love and be loved back.

Sam sighed. If she intended to tell her grandmother, she'd have to go to the ball also, and she couldn't do that in the clothes she had on. Her green hair had already created enough of a stir last night without wending through the formally attired in tee shirt and shorts.

She would go to her cabin and change back into her red dress. Then like Cinderella, she'd go to the ball.

Although unlike the story book character, she knew there would be no prince.

She'd find her grandmother and take her with her to wake up Jamie then tell them both together that she intended to leave the ship.

And go home where she belonged.

She belonged with Nate, her heart cried out in protest.

Not anymore, her brain replied just as fiercely.

\* \* \*

'There you are!' Ruby cried, calling to Sam over the heads of a dozen party goers. Ruby edged around the dancers spilling off the parquet floor and moved towards her granddaughter.

Sam's mouth went dry. She'd hoped to have a few more minutes, hadn't quite figured out what to say. But maybe it was better that way. Keep things simple, especially the lies.

She could only pray her grandmother's usual perception would be distracted by her occupation with Charlie, that Ruby wouldn't notice when Sam held back information.

'Jamie and I were looking for you all day,' Ruby chided. She peered anxiously at Sam's face as though expecting to find the answers there.

'Sorry Grams,' Sam replied. 'I had to go to town.'

'Shopping?'

'No. Work for Nate. I had some faxes to send.'

'They have fax machines on board ship.'

'They were private,' Sam lied, longing suddenly to throw herself into her grandmother's arms and sobbingly tell her everything. 'Nate thought it best not to send them from the ship. Besides we needed a computer.'

'Isn't your laptop a computer?'

'It didn't have the program I needed.' Why on earth was her grandmother choosing this moment to take an interest in new technology? She had always claimed in the past that computers held no appeal to a dinosaur like her.

'Then why bring it?' Ruby demanded. 'Charlie says — '

'Where is Charlie?' Sam interrupted.

'He popped down to his cabin to get the photos he developed today. He says there's a nice one of you and Nate standing at the railing with your heads almost touching.'

There'd be no touching anymore. Not now Nate was engaged.

'What does Charlie know about computers?' Sam asked, desperate to divert her thoughts from Nate. The lump in her throat grew larger.

'That's what he does, dear,' her grandmother explained.

'Computers?' Sam asked, unable to imagine her grandmother's old-world fiance involved in such a swiftly changing modern industry.

'Biggest distributor this side of St. Louis,' Ruby replied proudly.

'But I thought — '

'Thought what? That he sat on a

plantation and drank mint juleps all day?' Her grandmother chuckled. 'He likes to portray that image then he moves in like a shark and closes any number of deals.'

'Wow!' Sam shook her head. 'I guess I didn't really think about what he did. I was having enough trouble coming to grips with the idea of you having a gentleman friend.'

'Thought I was past it?' Ruby's eyes danced.

'No. It's just that he's so different from the men you know in Seattle.'

'If you mean they don't have his dash, his sense of adventure and humour, then you'd be right!'

'You really love him, don't you?' Sam whispered, wishing she, too, could express her love, that Nate could love her in return.

'I do,' her grandmother replied simply.

'Then I'm very, very happy for you,' Sam said softly. She put her arms around Ruby and gave her a swift hug.

'Thank you, dear.' Ruby hugged her in return. 'Once you get to know Charlie, you'll love him as much as me.'

'I'll look forward to that.' Her grandmother, at least, had found the best life had to offer. 'But how are you going to work things? You live in Seattle and he lives — where does he live?'

'In Virginia,' Ruby replied. 'He's asked me to come and visit him there when we get back from the cruise.'

'Oh!'

'I've told him I have to go home with you first and help find someone to care for Jamie while you're at work.'

'Don't worry about me and Jamie, Grams. We'll be fine.' Sam's mind raced, revising her plan. She'd take Jamie with her. Then her grandmother could go straight to Virginia if she wished, while she and Jamie returned to the life they were used to, the life before Nate. 'But what about you, Grams?' she asked, attempting a smile. 'Who's going to chaperon you?'

'I'm sure at our age, nobody thinks

we can get up to anything anyway,' Ruby replied, with a girlish giggle.

'What about children?'

'That's one thing I'm not worried about!'

'I meant does Charlie have any?' Sam asked, smiling in spite of the sadness eating away her heart. 'Has he been married before?'

'Never had time for it, he says. But it's something he now regrets. Especially since spending time with Jamie and seeing what a joy he is. He does have an older sister. Martha lives with their Aunt Sadie on an old plantation about a mile from Charlie's house. Charlie says it's all Martha can do to keep the ground floor tidy, let alone the rest of that big house. It's falling apart, by all accounts, but Sadie won't hear of having anyone in to do for them, says she'll go to her grave before she'll accept charity.'

'Charity?' Sam asked. 'Is she poor?'

'Pots of money, Charlie says. She just chooses not to spend it. Charlie wants the two of them to move in with him so that his sister can get a rest. He, apparently, has a housekeeper.'

'Where would you fit in?'

'Not as his housekeeper,' her grandmother replied with spirit. Then her voice lowered. 'I don't really know. I only know that he loves me as much as I love him, and that's all that really matters.'

'Not all,' Sam whispered, wishing her grandmother's words were true.

'What's happened between you and Nate?' Ruby asked gently.

'Nothing.'

'Then why do you look so sad? Even your hair has lost its bounce.'

'Weighed down by green dye.' Sam tried to smile, but failed.

'Talk to me, Sam.'

'It won't help.'

'A burden shared is a burden — '

'Not this time, Grams. There's nothing you can do.'

'So it is Nate?'

Sam pressed her lips tight to stop

them from trembling.

'Are you in love with him?'

As her grandmother spoke, the piano player on the bandstand rolled into a new song, a slower tune than the last, and very, very sensuous. As making love with Nate had been sensuous.

'Did you sleep with him?' Grams asked.

Sleep had been the last thing on their minds when they'd been in bed together, but, Sam realized dully, it was exactly what she needed now. The day had been exhausting, an aimless wandering around an island she didn't want to explore alone. She'd have to get used to that feeling again, because alone was where she had ended up.

Except for Jamie and Grams, who were as much a part of her as her own soul. If only she hadn't learned to want something more.

Someone more.

Nate.

'Talk to me, Sam,' her grandmother commanded.

'I did sleep with him,' she answered, her voice barely audible even to her own ears. The memory swept over her of tangled limbs and heat.

'So where is he now?'

'Getting married,' Sam whispered.

'To whom?' her grandmother demanded.

'To Fay.'

'He can't marry Fay!'

'They're perfect for each other. He wants a wife and she wants a man with money.'

'They don't love each other.'

'Love was never in Nate's plan.'

'Maybe not before, but that man loves you, Sam. I know he does.'

She had thought so too, had thought it with every fibre of her being. He may not have been ready to admit it, but the touch of his hand, the tenderness in his eyes, had all told her the truth.

And she loved him.

Like the clash of cymbals from the band on the stage, Sam realized she hadn't told Nate how she felt, hadn't said that she needed him and couldn't live life without him.

She had been a coward.

Not a word she would normally apply to herself. For even when Phil had left, leaving her young and alone, she'd cared for her tiny baby with love and strength. If she could be strong then, she could do it again now.

No matter what Nate decided to do, whether he married Fay or not, she had to tell him the truth.

She had to tell Nate she loved him.

'And you love him,' her grandmother added insistently.

'Yes,' she whispered, as a desert loved the rain.

'Then you've got to stop him from marrying Fay.'

'He's got to want that too.'

'He will when he finds out.'

'Finds out what?'

'That she's not who she pretends to be.'

'What do you mean?' Sam demanded. 'I know Fay!'

'I'm explaining this badly.' Ruby's

mouth twisted into a grimace. 'This afternoon Charlie, Jamie and I took the shuttle boat into town. Charlie had to make a phone call so we ducked into a little café, the Rainbow Café, I think it was called.'

'The name doesn't matter, Grams.'

'Jamie and I sat down at a booth while we waited for Charlie,' her grandmother went on. 'There was a woman in the booth behind ours. We couldn't see anything of her except for the top of her head.'

Sam glanced at her watch. If this was going to be one of her grandmother's long-winded tales, she'd never get back to St. Thomas in time to see Nate before the wedding. Eleven p.m., Fay had told her. It was ten-thirty already.

If she didn't talk to Nate, she would regret it for the rest of her life. She couldn't hope to change anything, but at least she would know she had the courage to say what needed saying.

'It was Fay,' her grandmother announced,

her voice lowering dramatically.

'What of it?' Sam asked. 'I may not be thrilled she's marrying Nate, but she's entitled to a cup of coffee.'

'You don't understand.' Ruby took hold of Sam's hand. 'I didn't until just now, when you told me she was marrying Nate.'

'Understand what, Grams?'

'There was a man with her and she was telling him that it would soon all be over, that by midnight tonight, she'd be a rich woman.' Ruby lifted her shoulders. 'I assumed she was talking about a New Year's lottery or something. I didn't realize — '

'Realize what?'

'That she was referring to marrying Nate.'

'I still don't understand — '

'She said by midnight tonight they'd have all the money they need.'

'Nate's inheritance.' Sam's stomach flipped. 'She's marrying him for his money.' The heat generated by the dancers had been hitting her in waves, but suddenly Sam felt cold. She'd suspected Fay's motives weren't the most honorable, but to hear that her old classmate had actually admitted that fact was unbearable.

'But she can't get her hands on Nate's money unless he gives it to her!' Sam exclaimed. 'He's not likely to do that, Grams. He needs that money for the business.'

'Never underestimate the power of a beautiful woman,' Ruby replied grimly.

Jealousy streaked through Sam. Even if Nate insisted otherwise, a marriage of convenience could very soon turn to passion, especially if that marriage involved a woman as attractive as Fay.

'I've got to go, Grams.' Sam's pulse throbbed against her temple. 'Jamie will be fine for a while. The sitter's with him until two.'

'Don't worry about Jamie.' Her grandmother tugged on Sam's hand and pulled her into an embrace. 'I'll take care of him. Just tell that young man you love him and make sure that he listens.'

'I will, Grams.' She hugged her grandmother tightly, suddenly more glad than ever that Ruby was in her life.

# 14

Sam considered then discarded the notion of changing before she went. There was no time, she decided, despite the difficulty of running in dancing slippers. Impatiently, she punched the elevator button, until finally, unable to bear the wait, she took the stairs instead. They might be no faster but at least she was moving.

Which felt good. Without movement, her courage might falter.

The same seaman still stood guard at the gangplank's head and he glanced curiously at her as he helped her aboard the shuttle boat.

'Last shuttle returns at three a.m.,' he informed her solemnly.

It would take only a heartbeat to say what she needed to say to Nate, to warn him about Fay and to tell him that she loved him. Her hands turned clammy at the thought of saying those words, but whatever happened when she told him, he had to know the truth.

If only the shuttle boat would move a little faster. It was approaching the shoreline with all the speed of a tortoise. Hugging her body with her arms, she watched the town's lights grow larger, and the people promenading along the shore grow more sharply defined.

Then the boat's engine cut and they were suddenly there. Before the seaman could affix the guy ropes and settle the gangplank into position, Sam had moved along it. She jogged toward the cabs parked along the kerb and stepped into the first in line.

'Where to?' the cabby asked, glancing dubiously at her in the rear view mirror.

'Justice of the Peace,' she answered softly, lifting her hand to her hair. Its green colour still jolted her as much as it obviously had the cabby. But maybe a jolt was what she needed to get through the next half hour.

'*Gov'ment* offices closed at night,' the driver informed her.

'Not tonight,' Sam replied. 'There's a wedding — '

'Getting married?' the driver asked.

'No,' she denied swiftly, but her heart pumped faster. 'I'm attending one.'

'*Gov'ment* offices closed,' the driver repeated then, wrenching his cab into gear, he pulled away from the kerb.

A sharp right, then a left, then a few swift blocks and they pulled up in front of a long, low building.

'Closed,' the driver said smugly, looking pleased to have been proved right.

'Perhaps there's a door around the side,' Sam suggested. She craned her neck to look.

The driver shrugged.

Sam reluctantly got out and handed him two fives. He took what she offered and sped off so swiftly his tires left a mark on the pavement.

She glanced at her watch. Five minutes past eleven. Her heart sank.

She was too late. The wedding would have already begun.

She peered through the frosted window to the left of the front door, but could see nothing, not even a light. She knocked anyway. When no one answered, she pressed her ear to the door.

There was a faint tinkle of music somewhere in the back. Sam reached down and removed a shoe, then pounded its heel against the door. A shuffling sound rewarded her efforts, and the door creaked open.

A stocky man whose white tee shirt was tucked half in and half out of his shorts stood in the doorway.

'Yes?' he said, banging the broom he was carrying against the wooden door sill. Dust drifted through the air and settled on Sam.

'A friend of mine was supposed to be getting married here tonight — '

'Don't know nothin' 'bout that. Ain't nobody here but me.' That said, he shut the door in her face.

She was left shoe in hand and nose hard against the door's grainy surface. Slowly she turned and balanced against the building to put her shoe back on.

Where was Nate? A wedding took longer than five minutes.

Although this wedding must be different. This wedding held no love. No flowers, no bridesmaids, no ringing of bells. Perhaps it could all be done in the blink of an eye, when there was no one to witness the insanity.

Sam closed her eyes against the winking neon light above the bar down the street and fought the despair welling up inside.

She was too late. Nate was married and gone with a woman he didn't love.

And she'd never have a chance to tell him how she felt, would never say the words I love you.

Her tongue felt thick with those unspoken words and her body awash with pain. Perhaps Nate had the right idea after all, for if this was how it felt to be in love, she wanted no more of it.

Sighing deeply, she opened her eyes. She couldn't stand here all night. What's done was done, as her grandmother often said. Best to face the fact Nate was married and move on as best she could. She had done it before. She could do it again.

Only this time it was harder. This time she felt an anger that nearly knocked her from her feet. Directed against Nate she had thought at first, but now she realized it was directed against herself. For allowing herself to care, for being sucked in once again to the maelstrom called love.

Pressing her lips tight, she moved toward the bar. She'd phone a cab from there, didn't trust her legs to carry her the few short blocks to the pier.

The air, at least, was warm, and it caressed her bare shoulders as a lover might caress.

As Nate had once, but never would again.

Pain shafted her again at the thought of Nate's touch, and she paused for a moment as she reached the bar, consciously pulling in and releasing the oxygen from her lungs. Then she pushed through the bead curtain covering the door, and strove to adjust her eyes to the dimness within.

The bar was empty except for a man sprawled in his chair with his back toward her, and a couple on the far side, the mini-skirted woman propped in her partner's lap.

The sorriest music she'd ever heard poured forth from the jukebox, something country and mournful and altogether too sad. She might have liked it at another time, but now all it did was remind her of Nate, of unrequited love, and a future faced alone.

She needed nothing more to remind her of that.

What she needed was a drink. The dryness in her throat had spread to the rest of her, leaving her parched and dehydrated and craving moisture.

Getting a cab could wait.

Wending her way past rattan chairs,

she reached the bar, climbed onto a stool, and motioned to the bartender.

'Perrier,' she ordered, 'and a glass of champagne.'

'We only sell it by the bottle.'

'A bottle will be fine.' It was New Year's Eve and she was alone, would probably always be alone. Might as well get used to it, start as she intended to go on, celebrate the beginning of a new year no matter how dismal the future.

The bartender pulled a bottle from the fridge and held it out for her approval. With an uncaring nod, she propped her chin in her hands and watched him unstop the cork. It flew from the bottle and landed across the room, directly in the drink of the man with his back to her.

'Sorry,' she muttered loudly, then turned away, watching as the bubbly fizzed up and over the sides of her fluted glass.

'Got one in there for me?' said a voice from behind.

'Nate,' Sam whispered, spinning on her stool.

'I didn't see you come in — ' He smiled his slow smile. ' — but when you started chucking things at me, I couldn't help but notice.'

Sam gripped the bar, her insides turning to jelly.

Nate reached forward and touched her shoulder. A current under water couldn't have packed more voltage. It sizzled through her body then must have boomeranged back to his, for Nate's eyes jerked wide as though struck by the connection.

'I wasn't chucking anything.' It was all she could do to keep her voice from cracking, from telling him everything that was in her heart.

'I just about chucked it back.' His lips tilted upward. 'Then I saw your hair and knew it was you.'

His voice told her he was glad. But he couldn't be glad. Not with things the way they were.

'Congratulations,' she said, the word

hurting her throat.

'For what?'

'Your marriage. Tonight, wasn't it?'

'How did you know?'

'Fay told me.'

His lips tightened.

'Where is Fay?'

'I don't know.' Then he reached for her again.

'Don't touch me,' she cried.

'I can't not.'

As she couldn't either. How had she ever supposed she could live without him, without his smile, his laughter, or the tenderness in his eyes?

The tenderness was still there, and it shouldn't be now. Not from a man who was married to someone else.

'After last night — '

'Last night should never have happened.'

'You don't mean that.' His shoulders bunched beneath his tuxedo jacket.

'I can't believe anything else.'

'You were there. You know how we felt.'

'It was nothing.' The lie held less pain than revealing the truth, but she had to know why he had done what he did, couldn't stand the not knowing. 'Why didn't you tell me?' she cried.

'I tried to tell you.'

'You said nothing.'

'You didn't want words.'

This was not her fault, this love without love. 'Fay said you were getting married tonight — '

'Yes.'

' — that you were engaged. She showed me the ring.'

'When?' His voice was suddenly sharp.

'This morning.' By twisting her head, she was able to hide her eyes and the fact that tears were forming there. 'I went looking for you,' she finished.

'You were asleep when I left.'

'Why didn't you stay?' She stared hard at him now, not knowing what his answer would cost her, simply certain she needed to know the truth.

'I had to see Fay — '

His words kicked her gut.

' — I needed to talk to her.'

'To tell her you were sorry?' Hurt spiralled through Sam.

'For what?'

'For sleeping with me,' she whispered.

'I'll never be sorry for that.'

She slid from her stool and stood ramrod straight. 'I knew how you felt about marriage, but I never thought you capable of this.'

'I need to explain.'

'There's nothing to explain.' She turned away, tripping in her haste on the railing at the base of the bar.

He grabbed her arm, steadied her. 'You didn't want to talk last night,' he said furiously, 'and you don't want to talk now. When do you intend to talk?'

'Never!'

'You've got to hear me out.'

'I'm not your wife, Nate. I don't have to listen to anything. That privilege belongs to Fay.'

'I'm not married to Fay.'

'You've still got time.' She tried to freeze her heart into stillness. 'Then you'll have everything you want; money, a loveless marriage — '

'That's not what I want.' He took her hand, his skin hot against hers.

'Where's Fay?' she asked again, desperately this time.

'I don't know.'

'The wedding was set for eleven.'

'That's what she said.'

'I saw the ring.'

'It was her mother's ring.'

So he hadn't bought it. He hadn't stood in the jeweller's shop and chosen it with quickened pulse. 'Not very romantic,' she whispered.

'Not romantic at all.'

'Which is what you wanted.' She said it to remind herself as much as to remind him.

'You don't know what I want.' His fingers tightened around her wrist.

'No romance,' she said, holding out her hand and folding over a finger as she ticked off the list, 'no real marriage, no children — '

His face whitened.

She longed to take back her words, to erase the hurt from his eyes.

'You can't trust Fay,' she added. That, too, would wound him but better to hear it now.

'What do you mean?'

'Grams saw her in town.'

'I've been looking for her all day.'

Because he loved her, Sam thought, her pain shafting deeper. 'Grams overheard her talking.' Sam locked her pain away. 'She's marrying you for your money.'

'She's not marrying me at all.' He gazed into her eyes, his expression all darkness and stark lines.

'Fay called it off?'

'I haven't seen her.'

'But you went looking for her,' Sam accused.

'I had to talk to her before I talked to you.'

'We have nothing to say.'

'I had to tell her — '

'Tell her what?'

'About you, of course.'

Sam's heart fluttered to life then just as swiftly died. He was sorry for what they'd done, wanted to make it right with Fay.

'Then I found out — '

'Found out what?' she asked dully.

'Who she is.'

'She's the woman you asked to marry you.'

'She asked me.'

'But you weren't averse to the idea,' Sam accused. 'I saw you kissing.' The image of that kiss still burned in her brain.

'We didn't kiss.'

'She had her arms around you.'

'She had just asked me to marry her. She slipped her mother's ring from her pocket onto her finger before I could say a word.' His eyes grew even darker. 'That's when you came in.'

'Looking a fright.'

'Looking beautiful.' He touched her hair. 'You still look beautiful.'

She wanted to pull away, tried desperately to find the strength. But she needed his touch as a seed needs the earth.

'She wasn't marrying me for my money,' he went on.

'Of course she was. She said so.'

His expression grew grim. 'Not when she could get so much more by not marrying me.'

'I don't understand.' Was it the fans twirling overhead that were making her dizzy or the Christmas lights twinkling in waves around the walls?

'She wants Uncle Edward's fortune for herself,' Nate explained. 'And it looks like she's going to get it.'

'What do you mean?'

'Who inherits Uncle Edward's fortune if I'm not married by midnight?'

'That historical society your uncle supported.'

'Fay is President of that society.'

'Then why did she agree to marry you?'

'What better way to stop me

marrying someone else?'

'She planned it?'

'Looks like it.'

Sam's body grew cold. 'I wonder — '

'What?'

'The dates I set up for you.'

His brows drew together.

'They kept falling through. The girl in the mud bath . . . Fay was in the Spa that day. Grams told me so. And some of the workers are inexperienced.' She gestured ruefully towards her own hair. 'It's easy to make a mistake if distracted.'

'Or bribed.'

'She wouldn't have!'

Nate shrugged. 'Could have worded it as a joke, or simply got the mud bath attendant talking.' He grimaced. 'Fay can stop anyone getting a word in edgewise if she puts her mind to it.'

'Is that why you didn't tell her no when she asked you to marry her?'

The room seemed to go still. Even the sweeping of the fans didn't raise any air. Sam looked at Nate as she waited for his answer and thought he'd never looked more handsome, or unreachable.

It was as though he was wrestling with inner demons and the demons were winning.

'You came into the room then,' he finally replied, 'and I couldn't tell her anything. I had to follow you.' His shoulders lifted. 'You know what happened then.' With a smile, he leaned towards her. 'We made love.'

'You left.' Even now the remembrance chilled her.

'Marry me, Sam.'

He'd asked her once before.

'Marry me,' he whispered again.

She couldn't breathe, couldn't think, could do nothing but stare. Into eyes so deep and black she could lose herself in their midst, but the light in their centres beckoned her onwards.

How could she say yes when he hadn't said he loved her, hadn't told her he needed her both as a woman and a wife, as a mother to children who would be siblings to Jamie.

She fought back the lump closing her throat. He didn't love her, didn't need her in any of the ways she needed him. He wanted her now because Fay hadn't turned up, and unless he married before the clock struck twelve, he'd lose his uncle's fortune.

'I can't,' she cried, and wrenched away, determined to leave before he saw her pain. After the love they had shared, how could he ask this of her?

'Sam!' he called after her.

She could hear his steps behind her as she raced towards the door, catching her as she went through it. Out on the street, there was no one but themselves. It seemed everyone else was indoors with friends and family, celebrating the New Year with joy and exhilaration.

She glanced towards the sky. If she could just see the stars, she'd have the strength to turn her back on this man that she loved. But a cloud had swept in, covering the stars and moon, shadowing Nate's face and wringing the light from his eyes.

'You can't run from this,' he growled.

'Why not? You did.'

'I'm not running anymore.'

'I'm not marrying you, Nate.'

'But you love me.'

He said the words softly, but their truth hit her soul. 'You don't love me,' she whispered in return.

'You haven't given me a chance to say that I do.'

'All you want is a wife so you can inherit your millions.' She pulled off her watch and shoved it in his face. 'Well you better keep looking. You've only got thirty minutes.'

'That's not what I want.'

'It's what you said.'

He touched her shoulder. 'I don't want to marry you by midnight — ' He put his arms around her. 'I love you, Samantha, and however long it takes for you to love me back, to trust me, is how long I'll wait.' He pulled her to his chest. 'We can get married tomorrow,' he whispered in her ear, 'or next week, or next month, or next year if that's what you want.'

She gazed up at him, heart pounding, and the clouds suddenly parted, bringing back the light. It was there in the sky and in his eyes . . . especially in his eyes.

'You love me,' she said wonderingly.

'Green hair and all.'

'But you know what I want.' She swallowed hard. 'What I need. A husband I can love — '

'You love me.'

' — and who loves me back. A husband who wants children, lots of them maybe, and who loves the son I've already got.'

'Any man would love Jamie.'

'It's not any man I'm talking about. It's you, Nate.' She forced the next words out. 'Jamie's own father left him. I can't risk that happening again.'

'I'd never leave him,' Nate said fiercely, 'but you're right. Jamie does need someone who can keep him safe.'

His jawline tightened. 'I can't promise to do that.'

'You're afraid.'

'We're all afraid of something.'

'You lost love once and you don't want to lose it again.'

'I don't want to lose you,' he said simply. 'Or Jamie.'

Sam linked her fingers around Nate's neck. 'You had no control over your baby's death, Nate. You can't blame yourself for that.'

'I'm trying hard not to do that.'

'I need a husband who believes.'

'You make me want to believe.' He laid his cheek against hers.

'A man I can depend on through good times and bad.'

'I won't let you down.'

'A man who doesn't leave.'

'That's one thing I can promise.'

'But you did leave,' she teased, a wild joy spiralling through her.

'Only to find Fay. Only to tell her I couldn't marry her. I don't know now how I thought I could marry someone I didn't love. I don't think if it had come to it that I could have gone through with it.'

'Even for twenty million dollars?'

'Tempting,' he said, but his eyes told her differently.

'A crazy plan,' she murmured, her words vibrating against his lips.

'It got me you,' he whispered back. 'I have Jenny to thank for that, and Uncle Edward.'

'What do you mean?'

'When Jenny was in labour and our baby died, when she realized she was dying too, all she thought about was me.' Nate's eyes grew bleak. 'Jenny told me she wanted me to be happy, that I was to find someone else to love.' He shook his head. 'I couldn't believe she was saying what she did, not when all my happiness was dying with her and my daughter.'

Nate's jawline tightened. 'That's when Jenny turned to Uncle Edward. He was standing in a corner of the hospital room, had come to rejoice with us in the birth of our child. Jenny's eyes seemed to burn. 'Make him,' she ordered.' Nate shook his head. 'My uncle looked at me and then looked at Jenny, then slowly, firmly told her he would.'

Nate brought his hand across his eyes, as though wiping away the scene. 'I didn't think about that after Jenny's death, couldn't imagine ever loving anyone else. I only worked. I was happiest doing that. I thought it was the only thing I could do in their memory.'

Sam wanted to kiss him, to hold him in her arms, to keep on holding and never let him go.

'It wasn't just Jenny that made my uncle do what he did. He'd been married once himself, before I was even born. He had loved her and she died. Mrs. Mulroy told me so.'

'Did he ever marry again?'

'No,' Nate said. 'He told me once he regretted that.'

'He must have been lonely,' Sam said softly.

'He was,' Nate replied, his lips brushing hers. 'I think that's why he loved having me around so much, although I didn't know it at the time. I think he realized as he grew older that he could have loved again, and when my wife died, he didn't want me to make the same mistake he had. He wanted me to experience all the love he had missed.' His gaze held hers. 'You're a gift, Sam. I don't think you know how much.' Then he captured her lips and for a long moment kissed her.

Sam revelled in his touch, felt his strength, his warmth, and the essence of his power.

'I love you,' he murmured against her lips and his love permeated through her, heating her inside.

She pulled away, gazed into his eyes. 'I love you, too, but you know that already.'

'You can say it to me every minute of the day. I want to hear it now. I want to hear it forever.'

With an intake of breath, she glanced

at her watch. 'There's still time,' she cried.

'All the time in the world.' He kissed her again.

'For you to marry me, I mean.'

He nuzzled her neck. 'Name the date.'

'How about tonight?'

He pulled away and stared at her as though she'd taken leave of her senses.

'If we hurry — '

'Hurry?'

'I can't wait,' she said firmly. 'If we're getting married anyway, why not do what your uncle wanted.'

'He'd be happy about that.' Nate's voice was low and husky. 'He was a romantic.'

'Like you,' she whispered back. 'But if we don't get a move on, Fay will win.'

His gaze searched hers. 'Are you sure, Sam?' he asked.

'With all my heart.'

He smiled at her then.

'Just think of how happy Mrs. Mulroy will be.' Sam matched his smile with a grin. 'And Samson.'

'How happy we will be. And Jamie.'

She took him by the hand. 'Think you can keep up?' she challenged, heading out along the road in the direction of the docks.

'What about a taxi?' he protested.

'No time,' she cried, pulling him into a run, her red dress hobbling her legs, shortening her stride. But down the narrow alleyway they flew, emerging as she had hoped at the dock along the seawall.

The shuttle boat was just revving up to take off, and the same sailor as before was pulling up the plank. The distance from shore to boat was short, and together, laughing, they leaped over the space.

'Had a good time, Miss?' the sailor asked, when they landed in the cockpit beside him.

'The best,' she said softly, conscious of Nate beside her and the love welling between them. 'We need to be back at the boat before midnight.' Her fingers tightened on Nate's. 'Will we make it?'

'Schedule says ten minutes before twenty-four hundred hours, and what the schedule says goes.' The sailor grinned. 'Or the officer on watch will throw us to the sharks.'

'Here's a twenty if we can get there earlier,' Nate offered, reaching into his pocket.

'Just send me a snap of your wedding,' the sailor replied, waving the money away.

'How do you know we're getting married?' Sam demanded, her heart leaping with joy at the thought.

'You both look as though you've been diving for treasure,' he explained, 'and have come up with gold doubloons.' He dropped his head shyly. 'Begging your pardon, ma'am. I don't mean to cast no aspersions on the colour of your hair.'

Sam smiled. Nothing could spoil what she was feeling inside, not even hair that looked as though it had been dipped in the sea until the colour stuck.

'My kid sister dyed her hair green,'

the sailor went on. 'Used juice crystals to do it.' He chuckled. 'My mom threw a fit, but my dad said it was a darn sight better than purple!'

'Purple,' Nate murmured, gazing thoughtfully at Sam's head.

'Don't even think it.' She lightly punched his arm.

'Anyway,' the sailor went on, as he wound up a rope, 'the two of you look to be in love.'

'We're hoping the Captain can marry us.' Nate looked at Sam as he spoke, his voice and eyes transmitting his love.

'I'll radio ahead,' the sailor offered, then left them to their embrace.

\* \* \*

She'd dreamed of this moment the whole of her life, but had never imagined it happening the way that it was, out here on the prow of a ship, under the eyes of God and family.

The first time she had married there had been a queasiness in her stomach she'd put down to pregnancy, but a part of her had known she was lying to herself, that she would regret her marriage more than anything she'd ever done. But she'd been too young and frightened to know Phil didn't love her, and that the evasiveness in his eyes should have told her he would bolt.

Even making their vows in a chamber at City Hall seemed as cold and loveless as the emotion in their hearts.

This time it was different. This wedding was like a fairyland filled with lights and loving family.

Sam glanced at her grandmother and found her face rapt with joy. She stood between Jamie and Charlie with a hand clasping each, but her gaze was fixed on Sam, her eyes bright with tears.

Jamie's eyes, behind his glasses, were filled with wonder and deep approval. When Nate had solemnly asked the boy if he minded his mother marrying him, Jamie had answered no so swiftly he'd stumbled on his words.

But it was the trust in Jamie's eyes

that clenched Sam's heart the most, and the hope that lit them like a beacon in the night.

'Do you, Nate Robbins — '

Sam's jerked her attention back to Nate.

' — take thee, Samantha Feldon, to be your lawfully wedded wife, to have, and to hold, from this day forward?'

Nate's eyes were all she saw now, and they were gazing at her. Slowly, lovingly, he recited his vows, his voice low and husky and filled with certainty. Sam felt now the love she'd waited her whole life to feel, and with it the commitment that would bind them together forever.

Then the Captain spoke to her and the world filled with light.

She gazed skywards and saw that the cloud had disappeared. In its place was a canopy of stars, with the moon in their centre beaming down in a shaft of gold.

As their marriage would be gold.

'I will,' she said firmly, in response to

the Captain's question. She placed her hand in Nate's, and the sound that she heard was not the silken strains of violins but the beating of her own heart as she joined her life with his.

## THE END

We do hope that you have enjoyed reading this large print book.

Did you know that all of our titles are available for purchase?

We publish a wide range of high quality large print books including:
**Romances, Mysteries, Classics**
**General Fiction**
**Non Fiction and Westerns**

Special interest titles available in large print are:
**The Little Oxford Dictionary**
**Music Book, Song Book**
**Hymn Book, Service Book**

Also available from us courtesy of Oxford University Press:
**Young Readers' Dictionary**
**(large print edition)**
**Young Readers' Thesaurus**
**(large print edition)**

For further information or a free brochure, please contact us at:
**Ulverscroft Large Print Books Ltd.,**
**The Green, Bradgate Road, Anstey,**
**Leicester, LE7 7FU, England.**
**Tel:** (00 44) 0116 236 4325
**Fax:** (00 44) 0116 234 0205

## A TENDER CONFLICT

### Susan Udy

Believing a local meadow to be the site of an ancient battle, Kristin Lacey and her small band of eco-protesters set up camp there in order to fend off ruthless property developer Daniel Hunter and his plans for 'executive' homes. Then Kristin discovers her mother has a secret that could put a spanner in the works — and, to make matters worse, she finds herself increasingly attracted to the very man who should be her enemy. When her feelings betray her, is she playing straight into his hands?

# CALIFORNIA DREAMING

## Angela Britnell

When plucky L.A. journalist Christa Reynolds loses her fiancé and her job, she decides it's time for a change of scene. Nearly seventy years ago, her English-born grandmother was evacuated from war-torn London to safety with the Treneague family in Cornwall, and as there's been a standing invitation ever since for the Reynoldses to visit, Christa decides to take them up on it. But she hadn't reckoned on meeting wounded ex-Marine Dan Wilson, and soon she has a life-changing choice to make . . .